'Move

'No,' she said, her chin up and her eyes glinting in the soft, low light. '... 'You show up in the early hours of New Year's Day, make a big deal about wanting to talk, and then suddenly you don't *want* to talk? You're making me worried and I won't let you leave when you're in this sort of state. So, come on—what gives?'

Now, clearly, was the time to march forward, physically lift her aside and make his escape, thought Kit, with the one brain cell that was still functioning rationally.

But that would mean being near her, laying his hands on her, he reasoned with the part of his brain that was addled with lust. And once that happened he wouldn't be lifting her out of the way but pulling her close, backing her up against the door and divesting her of her clothing.

Shoving his hands through his hair, he cursed whatever madness had made him think that seeking out his ex-wife had been a good idea.

Dear Reader

Lily Montgomery first made an appearance as Zoe's sister in THE REUNION LIE, when Zoe borrowed details of Lily's relationship with Kit to create her fictitious boyfriend. It subsequently turned out that after a whirlwind romance 'zany and creative' Lily had 'a brief but turbulent marriage' followed by 'the divorce to end all divorces'—and, while outgoing and fun, was deeply anti-men…her ex-husband in particular.

She sounded like an interesting girl, with a stormy past and an intriguing ex, and the opportunity to explore her and Kit's story was too irresistible to pass up.

So here it is: a tale about having a second stab at love and getting the rare chance to put right all the things that went wrong first time round. I hope you enjoy Kit and Lily's journey back to each other as much as I did writing it.

Lucy x

ONE NIGHT WITH HER EX

BY
LUCY KING

Harlequin (UK) ... started a policy ... to use papers that are natural, renewable and recyclable products and made from wood ... grown in sustainable forests. The logging and manufacturing process ... to the legal environmental regulations of the country of ...

Printed and bound in Spain
by Blackprint CPI, Barcelona

MILLS & BOON

Published in Great Britain 2014
by Mills & Boon, an imprint of Harlequin (UK) Limited,
Eton House, 18-24 Paradise Road, Richmond, Surrey, TW9 1SR

© 2014 Lucy King

ISBN: 978 0 263 91089 6

Lucy King spent her formative years lost in the world of Mills & Boon® romance when she really ought to have been paying attention to her teachers. Up against sparkling heroines, gorgeous heroes and the magic of falling in love, trigonometry and absolute ablatives didn't stand a chance.

But as she couldn't live in a dream world for ever she eventually acquired a degree in languages and an eclectic collection of jobs. A stroll to the River Thames one Saturday morning led her to her very own hero. The minute she laid eyes on the hunky rower getting out of a boat, clad only in Lycra and carrying a three-metre oar as if it was a toothpick, she knew she'd met the man she was going to marry. Luckily the rower thought the same.

She will always be grateful to whatever it was that made her stop dithering and actually sit down to type 'Chapter One', because dreaming up her own sparkling heroines and gorgeous heroes is pretty much her idea of the perfect job.

Originally a Londoner, Lucy now lives in Spain, where she spends much of her time reading, failing to finish cryptic crosswords, and trying to convince herself that lying on the beach really *is* the best way to work.

Visit her at www.lucykingbooks.com

Other Modern Tempted™ titles by Lucy King:

THE REUNION LIE

To the challenging, tough, frustrating,
wonderful, crazy thing that is marriage.

CHAPTER ONE

RIGHT. THAT WAS IT. Enough was enough.

As the last of Big Ben's twelve bongs echoed through the night and the sky began to explode with fireworks, Kit Buchanan knocked back the inch of whisky that was left in his glass and glowered at the dazzling display erupting over the Thames beyond the floor-to-ceiling windows of his penthouse suite.

Forget the work he'd lined up to do this evening; he hadn't touched it anyway. Forget the fact that it was the middle of the night and freezing cold; what with the burning sensation of the alcohol and the relentlessness of the thoughts drumming through his head he felt as if he were on fire.

And forget the fact that he was about to embark on a course of action that probably required a good deal more consideration than the ten minutes he'd just given it.

He needed to sort out the mess he was in. Now.

For five years he'd been suffering. Five long, torturous, frustrating-as-hell years, and he'd finally had it. He was through with the lingering guilt, the excruciating tension and the crippling anxiety, all of which vibrated through him pretty much constantly and all of which he'd had to live with for far too long. He'd had enough of beating himself around the head with more self-recrimination and regret than any man needed to experience in one lifetime.

And he was sick of having no option but to split up with the women he dated.

The last one, Carla, whom he'd been seeing for a month and with whom he'd broken up just a few hours ago, he'd liked more than usual. He wouldn't have minded seeing a bit more of her, seeing where the relationship might head.

But that was pretty impossible given the problem he suffered, wasn't it?

It really couldn't go on.

Kit slammed the glass down on his desk and made a quick call to commandeer one of his hotel's limousines. Then he grabbed his coat and strode towards the lift. He punched the little round button and waited, bristling with impatience as his mind churned with details of the trouble he had with sex.

For the first couple of years following his divorce he hadn't been too bothered by his inability to function in bed. He'd told himself that after what he'd done he'd deserved it, and would willingly take the punishment. He'd assured himself that it wouldn't last for ever, and that as he wasn't a hormone-ridden, sex-obsessed teenager he could live with it.

But depressingly—and worryingly—it *had* lasted, and when matters hadn't improved a year or two later he'd begun to get a bit concerned.

And while pride and the potential for total humiliation had stopped him from doing anything about it initially, eventually he'd gritted his teeth and summoned up the courage to make an appointment with his doctor.

Which hadn't helped in the slightest.

The doctor had told him that there was nothing physically wrong with him and had suggested that perhaps his problem was psychological. He'd recommended a course of therapy, which had been pointless largely because Kit hadn't been able to bring himself to be entirely open and

honest with the therapist about his relationship with Lily
or the circumstances surrounding their divorce.

After that he'd tried almost every option that was left,
astounding himself with the lengths he'd been willing to go
to to find a cure. He'd read books, scoured the Internet and
acquainted himself with homeopathy. Plumbing the depths
of desperation, he'd even given hypnosis a shot.

But he needn't have bothered with any of it because
nothing he'd tried had worked, and it had been driving
him nuts.

This evening, after he'd said a regret-laden goodbye to
Carla, he'd racked his brains for any course of action he
might have missed, *anything* that might help, and it had suddenly struck him that there *was* something he hadn't tried.

It wasn't guaranteed to succeed, he thought, his jaw
tight and a deep frown etched on his forehead as the lift
doors opened with a sibilant swoosh and he strode inside,
and God knew it wasn't in the slightest bit appealing, but
if the only avenue left open to him was to head straight to
what the therapist had suggested might be the source of
his problem—namely his ex-wife—and to see if talking
might work where everything else had failed, then that
was what he'd do, because frankly he couldn't stand this
affliction any longer.

'You're engaged?'

Lily leaned against the kitchen counter for support and
wondered what more the evening held in store for her in
the shock-to-the-system stakes, because if there was anything else waiting in the wings she was off to bed the minute she hung up.

'That's right,' replied her sister, her voice holding a
thread of excitement and happiness that should have been
infectious but for Lily, who held the institute of marriage
in deep mistrust, wasn't.

'Who to?'

'What do you mean, who to?' said Zoe, her laugh of disbelief echoing down the line. 'Dan, of course.'

'But I thought you'd split up.' With the hand that wasn't holding her mobile to her ear, Lily emptied the remains of the champagne bottle into her glass, and took a much-needed gulp.

'We had.'

'Didn't you say you were over for good?'

'I did. And I genuinely thought we were.'

Lily lowered her glass and frowned as she tried to make sense of what her sister was saying. 'So what happened?'

'Tonight happened,' said Zoe with an uncharacteristic dreamy sort of sigh. 'He came to find me.'

'Where are you?' Judging from the thumping music in the background it sounded as if Zoe was out, somewhere busy, which in itself was unusual given she spent practically every evening in cuddling up to her computer.

'I'm at a party.'

'A party?' Lily echoed, faintly reeling all over again because while going out in the first place was rare her socially inept sister had always considered attending parties a fate worse than death.

'I know,' said Zoe, her delight clear in her voice. 'Can you believe it? I can't. But anyway Dan showed up about an hour ago, rescued me from an overenthusiastic dance partner and then basically told me he realised what a jerk he'd been and apologised in the loveliest way imaginable. It was very masterful. Very romantic.'

There was a pause while Zoe presumably drifted off into a blissful memory of the moment before dragging herself back to the conversation. 'Then he proposed,' she added dreamily, 'and I said yes.'

Just like that? A few softly spoken magical words and Zoe had fallen headlong into Dan's arms? That didn't sound like her ever logical sister any more than dreamy romance did, yet there was no denying that it appeared that that was exactly what had happened.

Hmm, thought Lily, an odd ribbon of apprehension rippling through her. Tonight was turning out to be unexpectedly and oddly unsettling. 'But didn't you say over Christmas that you wouldn't take Dan back even if he were the last man on earth and he came crawling on his knees?' she asked.

'Did I?'

'You did.'

'Oh, well, that was then,' said Zoe lightly, as if the fortnight of tears and misery Lily had just mopped up had never happened, as if she hadn't swung between despair and fury like some kind of demented pendulum, as if she hadn't given her surprisingly large repertoire of four-letter words an extensive airing. 'But now it's all fine and we're engaged. Isn't it great?'

Lily took another gulp of champagne and thought that she wasn't so sure it was all that great. She'd been there, done that, and while she might not be the older of the two she was definitely the wiser when it came to marriage. In her brief but turbulent experience it wasn't all it was cracked up to be, as she'd spent the last half an hour only too vividly and infuriatingly remembering. 'But you've only known him, what? A couple of months?'

'Three.'

'Don't you think it's a bit soon?'

'You were married within six,' Zoe pointed out.

'And look what happened there,' said Lily darkly. A mere two years after they'd met and embarked on a whirlwind romance she and Kit had divorced. She'd married in haste and had ended up very much repenting at leisure. Not that she thought much about it these days. Normally.

'Dan isn't Kit,' said Zoe, beginning to sound a little defensive.

'I should hope not.'

'And I'm not you.'

'That's true,' Lily said, suppressing a sigh. 'You're a lot more level-headed and mature than I ever was. And older. But are you sure you know what you're doing?'

'Absolutely,' said Zoe with a quiet, firm certainty that Lily had never heard from her before. 'He's the best thing that's ever happened to me so be happy for me, Lil,' she added. 'Please?'

The plea was so soft, so sincere, so beseeching that Lily felt a sudden and unexpected wave of guilt and remorse sweeping through her. What was she doing? She was ruining what was the happiest night of her sister's life, and why? Because, unsettled by the last half an hour, she was only thinking about herself and *her* experience. What kind of sister was she?

Pinching the bridge of her nose, Lily closed her eyes and took a deep, steadying breath.

Just because she and Kit had made a mess of things didn't mean that Zoe and Dan would. Maybe her sister's would be one of the marriages that lasted. Dan was great, Zoe was great, so maybe they'd be fine. It happened, she'd heard.

And just because her night had nosedived and she'd been unexpectedly hit by a deluge of memories about what had been right about her own marriage and then a double whammy of regret and self-recrimination over what had gone wrong, that didn't give her the right to dampen Zoe's happiness.

Determinedly pushing her cynicism aside Lily pulled herself together. 'I am happy for you,' she said, pasting a smile on her face that she made sure her voice reflected.

'Really?'

'Really,' she said even more firmly. 'I'm sorry I wasn't more enthusiastic earlier. It was unexpected and I was just a bit surprised, that's all. Congratulations. I hope—no, I *know*—you'll both be very happy.'

'Thanks and we will.'

Lily heard the elation and the hope in her sister's voice and felt her heart squeeze. 'I think I might be the teensiest bit jealous,' she said. Because she could remember how Zoe was feeling all too well. The giddy happiness. The permanent grin. The excitement about the future…

'Are you all right, Lil?'

'I'm fine,' she said, to her irritation her voice cracking a little.

Down the line came a sharp intake of breath and the sound of the heel of a hand hitting a forehead. 'Oh, crap. Tonight's your anniversary, isn't it?'

What would have been her seventh. Not that she'd been counting. Until the clock had struck midnight and she'd been reminded of it at the most inconvenient moment imaginable. 'It is, but it doesn't matter.'

'Of course it does,' said Zoe. 'God, I'm sorry. And here's me banging on about Dan and getting engaged and stuff. I really am quite spectacularly insensitive. I should have thought.'

Lily shrugged as if it didn't bother her in the slightest. Which it didn't. Generally. 'Forget it.'

'Want to talk about it?'

'Nope.'

'Sure?'

'Quite.' She didn't want to even think about it, let alone talk about it, although that was proving annoyingly difficult to achieve this evening.

'OK, well, call me if you do. Any time. Really.'

Lily knew she meant it. Zoe had been a rock following

the divorce, and looking back Lily didn't know how she would have got through it without her. 'Thanks. I will.'

'Look, I'd better go. It's late and you have an early flight.'

'It is and I do.' A smile spread across her face at the thought of the week's holiday she'd booked following the week of work she had to do first. It would be the first holiday she'd had in ages and she couldn't wait. 'And shouldn't you be snuggling up to Dan instead of calling me?'

'Plenty of time for that later, I hope. Anyway, he's gone to get our coats and I wanted you to be the first to know.'

Lily's smile deepened. 'Thanks. You do realise that the second I get back I'll be grilling you for details?'

'You might regret saying that.'

'Never. I want to hear every single—'

The ring that reverberated through the silence of the house cut off her sentence and made her jump.

'What's that?' asked Zoe.

'Someone at the door,' she said, her smile fading and her heart sinking a little at the thought of who it might be. 'I should go.'

'Are you sure you ought to be answering it this late?' said Zoe, sounding like the older sister she was. 'I mean, I know there are first-footers and whatnot around, but you are on your own and it is well past midnight.'

'Don't worry, it'll probably be Nick,' said Lily, despondently pushing herself off the counter and heading into the hall. 'He left his scarf.' She'd texted him to say she'd put it in the post, but maybe, despite the disastrous outcome of the evening, he didn't want to have to wait that long and had decided returning to pick it up was a risk worth taking.

'Who's Nick?'

At the interest in Zoe's voice, Lily inwardly cringed because Nick was history, that was what he was. Unfortunately.

Earlier, however, he'd been the guy she'd invited over for

dinner. Nick was an interesting, intelligent, entertaining, good-looking man who made her laugh, and even though they'd only been on three dates she'd been ready to take things to the next level. Had *wanted* to take things to the next level, because from what she knew about him so far he seemed pretty much perfect: in addition to his favourable personality and looks, he didn't want children, he didn't make her pulse race and didn't appear to have any problem with communicating.

In her book those last few qualities especially made him an ideal future partner, hence the invitation to spend New Year's Eve with her.

The early part of the evening had gone swimmingly, and exactly according to plan. Nick had turned up on the dot of nine bearing a bottle of champagne and a warm smile that had turned even warmer when Lily had presented him with a deliberately lavish designed-to-seduce menu of four courses, vintage champagne and handmade chocolates.

Over the table and the next couple of hours they'd chatted easily and flirted outrageously, and things had been looking promising. Then they'd moved to the sofa in her sitting room to have coffee and chocolates in front of the roaring fire and at midnight he'd leaned forwards to kiss her.

And that was when everything had gone wrong.

The clock had been striking twelve and as Nick had drawn closer and closer she'd been suddenly and totally unexpectedly hit by a snapshot of her wedding day.

She hadn't thought about it for years, but around the sixth chime the image of her and Kit wrapped in each other's arms on the dance floor and kissing as they wished each other a happy new year was there flashing in her head as clearly as if it had happened yesterday.

The image had been deeply unwelcome—and not only because it couldn't have come at a more inconvenient moment—and she'd tried to blink it away. So much so that

Nick had eventually pulled back a fraction and asked her if she had something in her eye.

At that she'd stopped blinking, which hadn't been working anyway, and instead had told herself to ignore the memory and keep her focus one hundred per cent on the man next to her, who was leaning in once again for a kiss.

She'd studied his eyes wondering exactly what shade of green they could be described as, run her hands through his fair hair and then lowered her gaze to his mouth, but that hadn't worked either because within seconds she'd found herself imagining she was looking into the dark chocolate-brown eyes of her ex-husband, running her hands through *his* thick dark hair and kissing *his* mouth.

Then a bolt of desire had shot through her, her bones had begun to dissolve and her stomach had started to melt while her heart rate doubled.

Deeply unsettled by her body's behaviour, because first she was pretty sure the desire had nothing to do with Nick and second she'd spent the last five years deliberately avoiding that sort of head-screwing stuff and thus was *not* happy to feel it now, she hadn't been able to help jerking back a moment before Nick's lips touched hers.

Clearly and justifiably surprised, he'd sat back and frowned and asked what was up. She'd been so confused and disturbed by what was going on that Lily hadn't been able to do more than mutter an apology and something about having an early start.

Nick had said that in that case he ought to be making a move, and it was hard to say who was more startled when she jumped to her feet and thrust his coat into his hand practically before he'd finished speaking.

He'd left, sans the scarf, which in her haste to bustle him out had been overlooked, and she hadn't been expecting to see him again. Now it seemed she would, and what a way to round off New Year's Eve *that* was going to be.

'Never mind,' she muttered, because there was no point in Zoe being interested in who Nick was when she'd so well and truly screwed this evening and a potentially perfectly decent relationship up.

Zoe huffed. 'Never mind? That's all I'm getting?'

'Yup.'

'Hmm. Sounds like my engagement isn't the only thing we'll be having a chat about when you get back.'

Lily murmured something non-committal.

'OK,' said Zoe. 'Well, have a good flight and keep me posted about how it goes.'

'I will. I'll call you when I get there. And congratulations again, Zoe. I'm happy for you. I really am.'

'Thank you. Goodnight.'

''Night.'

Lily hung up and with a sigh dropped her phone on the table beside the spot where Nick's scarf lay folded, waiting to be stuffed into an envelope and put in the post. She plucked it off the table and through the frosted glass panels of her front door gloomily eyed the dark shape of a man.

Damn, she'd had such high hopes for him. Why, tonight of all nights, had the memories of Kit and their marriage managed to break through the impenetrable—she'd thought—barriers she'd erected? She'd done a pretty good job over the years of not thinking about her marriage, so why now could she think about little else?

Was it because this was the first year she'd actually spent the anniversary alone with a man instead of flinging herself around a dance floor in the company of dozens? Was it because she was stone-cold sober instead of rip-roaringly drunk?

And why hadn't she been able to suppress the memories and feelings even once Nick had gone? Why had they stormed round her head as if on some interminable flipping loop: images of Kit kissing her at the altar, feeding her wedding cake and holding her close as they danced; memories of the way she'd felt that day, how deliriously happy she'd been in the months that had followed and then how badly everything had imploded.

As a fresh wave of emotion rolled over her, her head swam and her throat closed over and she filled with an ache so strong her knees nearly gave way.

Well, if this was what New Year's Eve on her own or in the company of only one other was like she was never doing it again. Next year it would be hundreds of revellers and margaritas all the way.

Drawing in a shaky breath, Lily told herself to get a grip. All she had to do was open the door and hand over the scarf with, perhaps, an apology and the hint of an explanation.

Then she could take herself off to bed, bury herself under her duvet and hope that unconsciousness would take over until her alarm went off and she could busy herself with getting ready for the flight and work.

Simple.

Bracing herself, she pulled her shoulders back. She undid the latch and wrapped her fingers round the door handle. Then she pasted a smile on her face, turned the handle and opened the door wide.

She looked up.

And froze.

The greeting that hovered on her lips died. The apology she'd planned fled. Her smile vanished and her brain and body went into shock because the man standing on her doorstep, stamping his feet against the cold and blowing on his hands, wasn't Nick. It wasn't a first-footer.

It was Kit.

CHAPTER TWO

FOR A MOMENT Lily couldn't move. Couldn't breathe. Couldn't think.

All she could do was stare at him, her heart thumping too fast, the blood rushing to her feet and her head swimming with the effort of processing the fact that Kit, the man who'd made her happier and more wretched than she'd ever imagined possible, the man with whom she'd had no contact for the last five years but about whom she'd been thinking pretty much non-stop for the last half an hour, was here.

As shocks to the system went this evening this one was definitely the worst.

Half wondering whether her imagination might not have conjured him up what with the unauthorised way it had been behaving this evening, Lily swallowed, then blinked. Hard. Twice. She gave herself a quick shake just for good measure, but he was still there, tall and broad and as jaw-droppingly good-looking as he'd ever been.

More so, actually, she thought, flicking her gaze over him to give her time to gather her scattered wits. He'd changed in the last five years. Physically at least. He seemed bigger, more imposing somehow. He was only, what, thirty-two, but his dark hair was flecked with grey at the temples, and there were faint lines bracketing his mouth and fanning out from the corners of his eyes.

He looked harder, more cynical than she remembered

too. But then perhaps that wasn't surprising since she must have made life pretty tricky for him following the breakdown of their relationship.

Not that either the way he looked or his attitude to life was in the slightest bit relevant to anything any more. No, she'd got over Kit long ago, and she was now totally immune to looks that were overly good and attitudes that were dangerously and possibly attractively edgy, whoever they belonged to.

Still, she could really have done without seeing him this evening. Or ever again, for that matter.

'Happy New Year, Lily,' said Kit, his warm breath making little white clouds in the cold night air while his deep voice rumbled right through her and fired a tiny spark of heat deep inside her.

Which she *really* didn't need.

Damn.

Telling herself to stay cool and focused, and reminding herself that she was immune to voices as well as looks, Lily stamped out the heat and straightened her spine.

'What the hell are *you* doing here?' she asked, too on edge with everything that had happened tonight and too pissed off about the spark to bother about mollifying her words.

His eyebrows lifted at her bordering-on-rude tone. 'Expecting someone else?'

'Obviously.'

'Who?'

'The owner of this.' She lifted the scarf and he glanced down at it, a slight frown creasing his forehead.

'Nice,' he murmured, as well he might seeing as how it was one hundred per cent cashmere and enticingly soft.

'Very.' And she wasn't just talking about the scarf.

'Is he on his way back?'

'I doubt it.' Presumably the return of the scarf by post was fine.

'Then can I come in?'

'Why?'

'Well, for one thing it's absolutely freezing out here,' said Kit, turning the collar of his coat up and tugging it higher, 'and for another I need to talk to you.'

'About what?' As far as she was aware they'd said all they had to say to each other years ago.

'Let me in and I'll tell you.'

'I don't think that's a very good idea.'

'Why not?'

Lily frowned. That was an excellent question indeed. Logically there was no reason not to let Kit in. They'd been divorced for years, and it wasn't as if the experience had been particularly acrimonious or anything. It had been devastating and sad, of course, but in the end they'd both been so numbed by everything that had happened that they hadn't had either the energy or the will to fight it out.

In fact, the overwhelming emotion she could remember was a sort of resigned relief, because by the time they'd signed the papers there'd been nothing left and nowhere else for their relationship to go.

So logically she ought to give him a wide smile, stand back, wave him in and listen to what he wanted to say.

But then there was that damn spark of heat that was stubbornly and infuriatingly refusing to die.

If anything, it was getting stronger the longer she looked into his eyes, and that alone was reason enough to send him on his way because a spark was how this whole thing had started in the first place, and she was *not* falling under Kit's spell all over again.

Therefore he wasn't coming in.

'I'm sorry but I'm busy,' she said firmly.

He shot her a sceptical look. 'At half past midnight on New Year's Day?'

'Yes.'

'Doing what?'

'None of your business. Come back tomorrow.' When she'd be long gone.

'I'd rather get this over with now if you don't mind.'

'I do mind.'

'Can't we at least talk?'

Lily fought the urge to roll her eyes. Oh, the irony. Lack of communication was above all what had led to the breakdown of their marriage, and *now* he wanted to talk?

'When were we ever able to talk?' she asked with more than a hint of sarcasm.

As he contemplated her point, Kit sighed, then gave a brief nod. 'That's fair enough, I suppose. So how about you listening while I talk?'

'I don't remember that working either.'

'Doesn't mean it wouldn't work now.'

Lily folded her arms and lifted her chin. 'Doesn't mean it would.'

Kit noted both, and with a scowl shoved his hands through his hair, clearly deciding now not to bother hiding his exasperation at her intransigence.

'Look, Lily, it's been five years,' he said, sounding as if he was struggling to keep a grip on both his temper and his patience. 'Are you really telling me you don't think we can behave like rational, sensible adults about this?'

Rational and sensible? Hah. Reason and sense had never featured much in their relationship, and the clear implication that she was the one not being rational or sensible here seriously wound her up.

'Oh, I'm sure *I* can,' she said.

'Well, I *know* I can,' he said, his eyes glittering in the dark and taking on an intensity that made her breath go all skittery. 'So why are you so against us having a conversation? Can you really not even manage that? Haven't you changed at all?'

As the questions hit her one after the other, Lily reeled for a moment, stung at the accusation that she wasn't capable of conversation, then had to concede that he might have a point about the whole having changed thing.

She *had* changed. She was nothing like the spontaneous, adventure-loving, but possibly a bit self-absorbed girl who didn't have a clue how to handle what life was suddenly throwing at her she'd been at twenty-four. She was now responsible, successful and focused, and while she still made sure she had fun, the fun wasn't quite as abandoned as it once had been. She was also way more mature than she had been back then, and way more grounded. And she could converse with the best of them.

And if she'd changed, then why wouldn't Kit have changed too? After all, she'd read that he'd achieved his dream of owning a string of luxury hotels, which presumably meant that he'd overcome the very large obstacle she'd put in his way and had then set about putting all that nascent ambition she'd seen in him to good use.

From the other snippets of information she'd gleaned over the years—not that she'd specifically looked out for gossip about him or anything—she'd gathered that he was now regarded as something of a cool, ruthless operator in the business world, a man who was intuitive and decisive and rarely put a foot wrong. Given how keen he was to have this cosy little chat, he might even have learned how to communicate.

And as he said, it *had* been five years.

So maybe she was being a bit obstinate about this, and, dared she say it, childish?

Surely, despite their history, they could behave civilly towards each other? Surely they could talk, catch up even, without things descending into a trip down memory lane littered with bitter accusations, hurtful lashing out and pointless blame-laying?

Maybe she owed it to him to listen to what he wanted to say. In the dark days following their divorce she'd subjected herself to extensive self-analysis and had come to realise, among many other things, that she hadn't listened much during the latter stage of their marriage, and if he was here, now, it must be important.

Besides, if she continued to refuse, Kit might think she was protesting just a bit too much, and there was no way she wanted him thinking she was affected in any way other than being in shock at his appearance on her doorstep.

Plus it *was* Arctic out here.

And then there was her curiosity over what had brought him here. Despite her best efforts to crush it that was just about eating her up alive, so all in all what choice did she have?

'Fine,' she muttered. 'But it's late and I have an early start, so you can have ten minutes and no more.'

'Thanks.'

His expression relaxed and he shot her a quick, devastating grin that made her stomach flip, her heart skip a beat and that damn spark of heat flare up, all of which reminded her that she had to be careful. Very careful indeed.

Starting now, she thought, standing back and watching warily as he moved past her. She pulled back so that no part of him brushed against her, closed the door and tried not to think about the way the hallway she'd always considered rather spacious now felt like the size of a wardrobe and about as claustrophobic.

'Go on through,' she said, her voice annoyingly breathy. 'The sitting room's on your right.'

Following her instructions, Kit strode down the hall and into the sitting room. Lily put Nick's scarf back on the hall table and then followed him, assuring herself with each step that really there was nothing to worry about. She'd got over her marriage and Kit years ago and it was just the shock of seeing him after all this time that was making her react so oddly, that was all.

After taking up a position by the fireplace about as far away from him as possible, she watched him unbutton his coat, shrug it off and drape it over the arm of the sofa. He straightened, thrust his hands in the pockets of his jeans and looked around.

While the fire crackled merrily in the grate, she saw him take in the deep indentations in the cushions of the sofa, the pair of cups on the low coffee table in front of the fire and then, beyond the open doors that divided the space, towards the back of the house, the dining table upon which sat the evidence of what had clearly been a romantic dinner for two.

Surveying the scene through Kit's eyes, Lily knew what it looked like and was suddenly rather glad she hadn't got round to tidying up.

She was especially glad she hadn't done anything about putting out the dozens of flickering candles, turning up the low seductive lighting she'd chosen for this evening or switching off the slow, sexy music that drifted from the speakers embedded in the ceiling in the four corners of the room.

Why she was glad, though, was something she wasn't particularly keen to dwell on.

'You've been entertaining,' Kit said in a tone that suggested he didn't like it, which was tough because he'd given up the right to have an opinion about anything she did the minute he'd chosen to have a one-night stand with someone from the PR department of the hotel where he'd worked while their marriage lay in tatters.

Resisting the temptation to think about that, Lily allowed herself a slow, deliberately wistful smile. 'Yes,' she murmured softly, blissfully, as if dinner had turned into something much, much more.

Kit's jaw tightened gratifyingly. 'The man with the scarf?'

'That's right.'

'Boyfriend?'

Nope. Sadly. 'That,' she said, 'is none of your business.'

Kit tutted. 'Goodness, aren't we defensive?'

'I prefer "private",' she said, deepening her smile as she vaguely wondered what was stopping her from just telling him the truth about Nick.

'So I recall,' he said, and in that instant an image flashed into her head of the two of them in his car, hidden from view, she'd thought, by trees.

They'd been driving back from a party in Kit's convertible, and it had been end-of-the-summer hot. He'd said something that she hadn't caught, and as she'd turned to ask him what he'd said she'd been hit by a bolt of desire so strong that it had wiped her head clean of thought. He'd looked so mouth-wateringly gorgeous, tanned and laughing, with the wind ruffling his hair, so confident and in control, that, totally riddled with lust, she'd ordered him to pull over.

Once he had, in a conveniently secluded spot, she'd practically leapt on him. Kit hadn't complained, and with their mouths meeting and their hands grappling at relevant bits of clothing they'd been too desperate to notice the group of walkers heading along the path in their direction, and then too absorbed in each other to see them hurry straight past.

It was only when Lily lifted her head from the nook where his neck met his shoulder, eased herself off him and turned to face forwards, that she saw the backs of a few stragglers and realised what had just happened. After that mortifying experience, Lily had insisted on sex indoors.

Why Kit had had to bring it up now she had no idea, but

she really wished he hadn't because she could so do without the memory of it. Or the accompanying rush of heat that was sweeping through her.

She could definitely do without the faint knowing amusement with which he was looking at her that suggested he knew exactly what was going through her head.

Hmm. Maybe it wouldn't be such a bad thing for him to believe she had a boyfriend. If her immunity to him wasn't quite as strong as she'd always thought and if he was even *thinking* of continuing with this line of conversation, then a boyfriend seemed like an excellent deterrent/defence.

Lily shrugged away the images. 'Well, it's early days,' she said with a coolness that came from who knew where. 'With Nick and me, I mean. But yes, things are looking good.'

'Great,' he said, sounding as if he thought it anything but.

Snapping his gaze from hers, he glanced down at the glasses that were on the coffee table and frowned. 'Are those ours?'

The crystal champagne flutes had once upon a time indeed been theirs, although now, technically, they were hers. They'd been a wedding present, and until tonight had spent the last five years encased in bubble wrap and stashed in her attic.

Lily wasn't entirely sure why she'd brought them down and unwrapped them this evening, but she had, and that had been a mistake because every time she'd lifted hers to her mouth she'd been hit by a string of bittersweet memories of drinking champagne with Kit.

'I have no idea,' she said with a dismissive shrug because there was no way she was going to confess to any of *that*.

'Looks like they are.'

'Does it matter?'

'It does if you're drinking out of them with another man. I think I might be offended.'

She fought the urge to bristle and channelled her inner calm instead. 'Well, you could have had them, so you should have thought about that when you displayed so little interest in how our things were divided up.'

He nodded and rubbed a hand along his jaw before shooting her a rueful smile. 'I probably should have. Although from what I remember I was too devastated by the realisation that we were over to be worrying about who got what.'

Lily stared at him in astonishment, all pretence of cool detachment gone. 'You were devastated?'

'Of course I was.' He said it as if she should have been able to tell, but by that point he'd been so cold, so distant, so damn unreadable that she hadn't been able to work out what he'd been thinking. 'Weren't you?'

'Oh, well, yes, I was in bits.' Which she'd clearly done a pretty good job of hiding too, if he'd had to ask. 'Although I do remember, above all, an overwhelming sense of relief.'

He nodded. 'Yes, there was that too.'

Silence fell then, and all she could hear as they continued to look at each other was the ticking of the antique mahogany clock on the mantelpiece. And all she could suddenly—and irrationally—think was, had he really been as devastated as she'd been? Had they been too quick to divorce? Should they have tried harder? Should they have given it another shot?

The clock struck a quarter to one and she came to with a jolt.

No. They could have given their marriage a million different shots but it wouldn't have made any difference because before divorce had ever been mentioned, before Kit's one-night stand even, they'd totally lost the ability to

communicate and their relationship had gone way beyond
the point of no return.

With her throat beginning to ache with regret Lily
quickly reined in her thoughts and pulled herself together.
She swallowed hard and perched her bottom on the ledge
of the built-in cupboard to the left of the fireplace.

Maybe they'd be better off focusing on the present and
why Kit was here. And come to think of it…

'How did you know where I lived?' she asked, curious
and now a bit suspicious because she'd moved a couple of
times before buying this place, and the forwarding address
of the flat she'd rented after their divorce had been out of
date for years.

He blinked and gave his head a quick shake as if he too
had been lost in thought. 'I have for a while.'

'That doesn't answer the question.'

'Doesn't it?'

'Have you been checking up on me?'

'From time to time.'

'Why?'

'I'm not sure.'

Lily didn't know what to make of that. 'Am I supposed
to be flattered?'

'Not remotely.'

'Good.' Because she wasn't. Not even a little bit. Truly.
'Then why didn't you just call?' Presumably if he had her
address he also had her phone number.

'It's late.'

'Or email?'

'Couldn't wait.'

'Sounds like you were desperate.'

'You have no idea,' he muttered.

'You're right. I don't,' she said loftily, as if she was way
above desperation when it came to him.

At her tone, a small smile played at his mouth. 'This is a nice place.'

'Thank you.'

'You've done well.'

She'd done more than well. Following their split she'd jacked in her marketing job and set up her own business, asking her sister—practically the only person she'd been able to trust—to run it with her.

At the time it had saved her. Been something of her own, something that had belonged to her and she to it, and she'd desperately needed it. That the two of them had been so successful had been unexpected, although of course greatly welcome.

'I think so. So have you.'

Kit's smile faded and he tilted his head as he fixed her with a look designed to make her feel uncomfortable. Which it did. 'In spite of your best efforts to sabotage me.'

Lily inwardly cringed. When Kit had broken down and confessed to having a one-night stand she'd cut up his suits and scratched his car and then fired off an email to every one of the institutions he'd been planning to seek financial investment from, telling them in no uncertain terms exactly the sort of man they'd be backing. It must have made things difficult for a while to say the least.

'Are you here for an apology?' she asked, because although it seemed unlikely it wasn't beyond the realms of possibility, she supposed.

'If I were would I get one?'

She bit her lip and nodded. 'You might.'

His eyebrows rose. 'Seriously?'

She gave a nonchalant shrug as if she hadn't been racked with guilt for months afterwards. 'Well, like you said it has been five years and maybe with hindsight I've realised that what I did was unforgivable.'

He held her gaze steadily and to her dismay she felt the

beginnings of a blush. 'I guess you did have some justification,' he said. Then, 'It was what I did that was the truly unforgivable thing.'

For several long moments, there was utter silence and the air began to thicken with a tension that Lily really didn't want to explore.

It would be so easy to slip into a painful post-mortem of their marriage but what good would that do? While time had healed the wounds no amount of talk would wipe out the scars, and picking over the bones of their relationship was the last thing she wanted to do when she was feeling so out of sorts. Or ever, for that matter, because she'd done plenty of it at the time. She certainly wasn't about to launch into a full confessional about how she'd come to acknowledge her role in the breakdown of their marriage.

Besides, presumably Kit was here for a reason, and one that in all likelihood didn't involve raking up the past.

'So why now, Kit?' she asked. 'After all this time? Why the urgency? Why are you here at nearly one in the morning on New Year's Day?'

He rubbed a hand over his jaw and began to pace and she got the impression he was nervous, which was odd because nervousness wasn't a state of mind she'd ever associated with him. Even when they'd waited for the results of the endless pregnancy tests she'd taken, when she'd been a bag of nerves, gnawing on her nails and practically quaking with hope and dread, he'd sat there stonily tense, looking more impatient than anything.

'Could I get a drink?' he said, suddenly stopping midpace and whipping round.

Lily snapped out of it and stood. 'Sure. Sorry. What would you like?'

'Whatever you've got. Something strong.'

She went to the drinks cabinet, took out a bottle of brandy and filled a glass. Then she handed it to him, watched as he knocked it back in one swallow and felt a flicker of alarm.

'That bad, huh?' she said with a small frown, her resolve to stay strong and aloof wobbling a bit at the realisation Kit wasn't quite as in control of himself as she'd thought.

'Pretty bad.'

'Are you ill?' she asked, and braced herself.

'Not exactly,' he muttered.

'What does that mean?'

She held up the bottle in case he wanted another but he shook his head and set the glass down on the table. Then he straightened, shoved his hands through his hair and frowned down at a spot on the floor. 'It's complicated,' he muttered.

Lily stashed the bottle back in the cupboard and stifled a sigh. It always was complicated with Kit, but then she wasn't exactly Miss Simplicity herself. Together, not talking, not listening, not really knowing each other all that well, they hadn't stood a chance.

'OK, Kit,' she said, moving to the sofa and hoping that this wasn't going to be too traumatic and that she wasn't going to regret not standing her ground and sending him away when she had the chance. 'If you want to talk, then talk.'

CHAPTER THREE

IF KIT HAD had any doubt that his troubles were bound up with his ex-wife, it vanished the second Lily sat down on the sofa.

On the drive over he'd told himself that he was wasting his time because why would going to see her work when everything else had failed? What exactly was he after? Forgiveness? Understanding? What made him think she'd grant him either now when she'd been so unforgiving and so *un*-understanding at the time?

She probably wouldn't even be in, he'd thought. The Lily he'd known had been a party animal and tonight, after all, was one of the greatest party nights of the year.

But the soft golden light shining through a gap in the curtains drawn across the window at the front of the house had suggested she was at home. And that was when Kit had sent his driver home because, even though he was most definitely not looking forward to it, having come this far he wasn't about to back out.

It was that thought, along with the strong sense that he was nearing the end of his tether, that had kept him standing there on her doorstep when every defensive bristling inch of her was telling him to go.

It was that thought that had made him ignore her initial reluctance to engage with him, her subsequent spikiness, the occasional flash of temper he caught in her eyes and his strong yet totally irrational and unfathomable dislike of the fact that she was in a relationship.

Everything that had been said or hinted at as well as the simmering undercurrent of tension that had been running beneath the conversation of the last half an hour had taken a back seat to the need to get her to listen and the hope that his 'problem' might be about to be solved.

Now, though, his brain was clearing of that too because Lily was sitting down and settling back and crossing her legs, a move that made her dress ride up and exposed a length of thigh.

And suddenly, the memory of how soft her skin felt beneath his hands and his mouth, how tightly she used to wrap her legs around his waist whenever they made love, flashed into his head and, without warning, a wave of lust crashed over him so hard and fast it made his entire body shudder.

Before he had time to recover from the shock of that he was then hit by a whole load of other things that up until that point he'd been too distracted to notice. Such as the way her dress was so tight that it looked as if not a square millimetre of it could bear not touching her. Such as the glorious sheen of her hair, the mesmerising green shimmer of her eyes, the heavenly curves of her body.

He ran his gaze over her and he jolted as if he'd just been plugged into the national grid. Nerve endings that had been dead for so long tingled and quivered and his head pounded with such need he could barely remember his name let alone what she'd just said.

Clearly expecting him to fill the stretching silence, Lily arched an eyebrow and folded her arms beneath her breasts, pushing them together and up and making them swell over the bodice of her dress.

Kit was mesmerised by the movement. His mouth watered, his pulse raced and the sudden urgent desire to haul

her into his arms and tussle her to the floor nearly wiped
out his knees.

Just as had happened the first time they'd met.

Lily had been on a skiing holiday with friends and so
had he. She'd been whooshing down the mountain like a
pro, and he'd found himself watching her from the bottom
of the slope in admiration. Until towards the bottom she'd
lost control, crashed straight into him and together they'd
pitched headlong into a snowdrift.

Winded and stunned, for a second they'd just lain there,
struggling for breath, their hearts thumping against each
other. After a moment, still sprawled on top of him, her
eyes sparkling and her cheeks flushed, Lily had started to
apologise, but then her gaze had met his and the apology
had died on her lips.

It had been the epitome of madness, but despite the cold
snow surrounding them chemistry had taken over, heat and
lust had flared between them and within seconds they'd
been kissing. Devouring each other. Rolling over so that
he was pinning her to the ground, while she wrapped herself around him and nearly made him forget that they were
in public.

Now he was remembering how wild she'd been in bed,
how responsive, how hot and explosive they'd been together before everything had started to go wrong. And as
the memories began to come hard and fast all his blood
shot south, and within seconds he was sporting an erec-
tion harder than granite.

Great, thought Kit, beginning to sweat as the throb-
bing in his body strengthened. No proper action in that
department for five long, dry, frustrating years, and yet
one glimpse of Lily's thigh, a hint of soft, luscious cleav-
age and there it was. His libido, back with ferocious force.

He shoved his hands deep in his pockets as much to stop
them from reaching out to strip that dress from her body

and touch her as to disguise the very visible effect she was having on him.

'Well?' she said expectantly, and he stared at her mouth, desperate to find out if she still tasted the same, felt the same.

Which he couldn't do, he realised as common sense made a timely and most welcome appearance. For about a billion reasons. She was his ex. He hadn't thought about her like that for years. She probably still hated him. He didn't think he particularly liked her. They had more history than the Egyptians. She had a boyfriend. He wasn't thinking rationally. Or with his head.

In fact, he should probably get out of here. Now. Before he lost control and did something he'd regret. Which was all too possible given the length of his abstinence and the strength of the assault his body and mind were under.

'I should go,' he said, his voice sounding scratchy and rough.

Lily stared up at him in baffled astonishment. 'What? Go? Why?'

'You were right—we don't have anything to talk about.'

So much for all that nonsense about being able to behave like rational, sensible, civil adults, thought Kit grimly. Right now he was feeling anything but.

'Really?'

'Really.'

She frowned. 'Are you all right, Kit? You seem kind of upset all of a sudden.'

The effort of keeping himself under control what with everything that was raging inside him was making his jaw ache. 'I'm fine.'

'You don't look fine.'

'Leave it, Lily.'

'I don't think I can,' she said. 'You really don't seem well.'

'I'll survive.'

Once he was out of here and out of her head-wrecking orbit and once he had time and space to work out what was going on he'd be absolutely fine.

Probably.

Galvanising into action, Kit grabbed his coat and began to shrug it on.

'Wait,' she said urgently. 'Was it something I said?'

The concern in her voice only made him feel even more confused. 'No.'

'Something I did, then?'

Out of the corner of his eye he saw her frown and bite her lip and he gritted his teeth against the urge to throw himself on top of her and kiss the life out of her.

This was horrendous. Why her? Why now? he wondered, his head pounding. He'd met dozens of women over the last few years. Beautiful, intelligent, fun women. Many just as attractive as Lily. Some even more so. So what the hell was happening here?

'It *was* something I did,' she said, leaping to her feet and taking a step towards him, potentially so close that he violently recoiled before she could touch him.

'Don't,' he snapped.

Lily froze. She paled. Frowned. Then said a bit shakily, 'What's going on, Kit?'

'Nothing.' Why wouldn't she shut up and let him get on with the business of leaving?

'Rubbish.'

Kit ignored her. She could be as sceptical as she liked. He didn't care. He was off.

Not bothering with buttons, he whirled round and made for the way he'd come in, but before he could stride down the hall, through the front door and out into the safety of the dark, cold night Lily had whipped past him and planted herself between him and escape.

He stopped in his tracks while she stuck her hands on her hips and set her jaw, a stance he'd never seen before but suggested she wasn't going to let him go without an explanation. Which he was damned if he was going to give, so if she didn't budge he'd just have to lift her out of the way.

'Move, Lily.'

'No,' she said, her chin up and her eyes glinting in the soft, low light of the hall. 'You show up in the early hours of New Year's Day, make a big deal about wanting to talk and then suddenly you don't want to talk? You're making me worried and I won't let you leave when you're in this sort of state. So come on, what gives?'

Now, clearly, was the time to march forwards, physically lift her aside and make his escape, thought Kit with the one brain cell that was still functioning rationally.

But that would mean being near her, laying his hands on her, he reasoned with the part of his brain that was addled with lust, and once that happened he wouldn't be lifting her out of the way, but pulling her close, backing her up against the door and divesting her of her clothing.

Shoving his hands through his hair, he cursed whatever madness had made him think that seeking Lily out had been a good idea.

And then, beneath his breath, he cursed *her* because why the hell was she making such a big deal about this? Why wasn't she just letting him leave? Why did she care what was going on inside his head?

Come to think of it, why was *he* making such a big deal about this? Why was he getting so wound up by what was happening to him?

He ought to be glad his problem seemed to be solved, that he was 'cured'. He ought to be thanking her and heading to the nearest bar in search of someone with whom he could make up for lost time. Or calling Carla, perhaps.

And so what if he was still attracted to Lily? There was

nothing surprising about that. The chemistry that had existed between the two of them had always been instant, fiery and intense. Even towards the end of their relationship when they'd been too battered by what had happened between them to want to act on it, it had still been there, simmering away in the background.

But what if what he was feeling towards Lily now was more than mere sexual chemistry? Something deeper?

Kit froze as the idea of this stormed into his mind and opened up a whole labyrinth of other possible truths.

What if the problem he'd had sleeping with other women in the last five years didn't have anything to do with guilt or regret or self-recrimination? What if it was down to the fact that he was still hung up on his ex-wife?

He'd assumed he'd got over Lily years ago. But from the moment they'd met she'd got under his skin and been in his blood, like some kind of fever, the sort that was quick, fierce and lethal. And incurable. So maybe she was still there. In his blood. Under his skin. Tucked away in some long-forgotten corner of his heart.

Maybe that was why he'd kept vague tabs on her. Maybe that was why the idea of her having a boyfriend bothered him so much. Why he'd wanted to remind her of the good times they'd had together and had deliberately if obliquely brought up that afternoon in the woods.

Maybe she still felt something too, he thought, his heart hammering while his mind churned. Hadn't she flinched when she'd let him in? Hadn't her eyes darkened and her cheeks reddened when he'd alluded to the al fresco sex?

Despite the cool-as-a-cucumber air she was exuding now, despite the defiant stance, he could hear a slight shallowness to her breathing and he could just about make out a familiar faint flush to the skin of her upper chest. There was also a flicker of heat in her eyes that he didn't think was solely down to her wish to know why he was here.

So maybe, as chemistry didn't seem to have a time limit any more than it had anything to do with liking and trust, she was still as attracted to him as he was to her. Maybe it was something more for her too, despite the existence of a boyfriend.

Maybe he ought to think about finding out.

With his common sense spinning off into the distance and his head swimming with need, Kit abandoned what little remained of his self-control and took two steps towards her.

He stopped half a foot in front of her, so close he could smell her scent, could feel her heat, could feel himself helplessly begin to respond to the magnetism that had always pulled at them.

'Is whoever he is really your boyfriend?' he asked, looking down into her eyes, his mouth dry and his body wound so tightly it was in danger of shattering.

Lily blinked, clearly taken aback. 'Nick?' she said, her breath catching and a pulse hammering at the base of her neck.

'Yes.'

Her eyes widened. 'Is that what this is about, Kit? Do you suddenly have a problem with me moving on or something?'

'Possibly,' he muttered because, as disconcerting and unexpected as it might be, he suspected he did.

And then her eyes narrowed and filled with indignation, and she pulled her shoulders back and glared up at him. 'Well, that's just tough because you don't get to have a say in what I do any more. You don't get to have an opinion. And you certainly don't get to comment on my boyfriends.'

'I know that,' he said roughly, trying but failing to ignore the implication that there'd been a few.

'Anyway, would it be so hard to believe if he was?'

'Not at all.'

'Good.'

'Disappointing as hell though.'

She arched an eyebrow and tilted her head in challenge. 'Oh, really? Why?'

The provocative stance, the energy emanating from her and the flurry of memories that were now shooting round his head killed off the last remnant of his self-control, and Kit felt himself begin to unravel.

'Because even though I know it would be mad,' he said, his voice hoarse with the effort of restraining himself, 'even though I know we haven't seen each other for five years and have enough baggage to sink a liner, I'm this close—' he held his thumb and forefinger a centimetre apart '—to dragging you into my arms and hauling you off to bed. The only thing that's stopping me is this boyfriend of yours and even he's now beginning not to bother me. So if you have any sense of self-preservation whatsoever, if you don't feel the same way, then I suggest you step aside and let me leave. Now.'

As the words sank into her head Lily's mind reeled and her heart lurched. Kit wanted to take her to bed? Could she really have heard that right? Surely she must have got it wrong. Surely his proximity was having such a disturbing effect on her mind and body that she'd misheard or something because the very idea of it didn't make any sense at all.

Kit hadn't given any indication of wanting her earlier. Quite the opposite, in fact. He'd been cool and utterly indifferent to her. Which was entirely to be expected. They hadn't seen each other in five years and didn't even like each other particularly.

But no, she thought, blinking up at him in astonishment. It seemed to be that she hadn't misheard and he really had just told her that he wanted to sleep with her. She could see it in his dark eyes, blazing down at her with barely suppressed desire, and she could feel it in his body, which was radiating heat and vibrating with tension.

And even though it could well be nothing more than a simple case of male jealousy or a misguided attempt at marking out territory or something, whatever it was, for one brief, crazy moment she wanted to throw caution to the wind, fling her arms around his neck and sink into him because it had been so long since she'd had great sex and she missed it more than she'd ever let herself admit.

But she stamped out the temptation, set her jaw and held her ground. She hadn't spent the last five years of her life building up sky-high defences to protect herself against men who could cause her the kind of emotional turmoil he could only to have them annihilated by the very man who'd created her need for them in the first place. She'd trained herself to look forwards, not back, and Kit didn't feature in her present, let alone her future.

She didn't want to sleep with him anyway, she told herself firmly. She was totally over him and completely immune. In fact she rather thought she was appalled, insulted and even disgusted by his suggestion.

Especially if *this* was why he'd come here. Lily frowned as the possibility crossed her mind. Was it? Was he on some sort of booty call or something?

Well, if he was, she thought, her indignation firing, that was just awful. If he was, she'd have liked to be able to turn back time in order to slam the door in his face when he first pitched up on her doorstep.

'You want to take me to bed?' she said, her tone as scathing as she could manage, which wasn't very because in amongst the indignation and shock was something that felt suspiciously like hurt, although what there was to be hurt about she had no idea.

'Very badly.'

'Why?'

'You have to ask?'

'Clearly,' she said dryly. 'Are you lonely for a little company on New Year's Eve, Kit?'

'Perhaps.'

'You must be pretty desperate if you're here.'

'I am.'

'So what is this? Auld lang syne and the remembering of old acquaintances or something?'

'I don't know what this is,' he muttered, shoving his hands through his hair, looking as baffled as she felt. 'I didn't come here to sleep with you, Lily, but nevertheless I want to.'

'Well, I don't, so dream on, darling, because it's never going to happen.'

He nodded. 'Fine. Then move aside and I'll go.'

'Right.'

'You aren't moving.'

'I'm about to.'

But she wasn't. Because, to her horror, her feet refused to move.

A burst of panic exploded inside her and she felt a cold sweat break out all over her skin.

Why wasn't she sending him on his way, as he'd demanded? Why wasn't she moving aside, wrenching the door open and bundling him out? Why was she still standing here, deliberating, struggling with herself?

Struggling with herself?

Oh, no, she thought, her heart hammering. Why was what should be an easy decision a struggle? Why was she dithering? She wanted him to leave, didn't she? She didn't care why he was here, did she? She was over him. Wasn't she?

Kit went very still, alert, like a panther about to pounce. 'You still feel it too, don't you?'

'Feel what?' she said, so poleaxed by the notion that she even had to question her indifference to him after such certainty for so long that for a moment she genuinely didn't know what he meant.

'The chemistry.'

'I don't know what you're talking about,' she said, not altogether genuine now.

'Yes, you do.'

'I'm over you,' she said to convince herself more than him.

'Are you?'

'Totally.'

'Then why aren't you moving?'

'You're in the way.'

He took a step back, but to her alarm it didn't make any difference to her mobility. And he knew it. She could tell by the glint in his eye, and the panic escalated to such a level that she thought the top of her head was about to blow off.

What if she wasn't as over him as she'd thought? What if, despite all this time, despite all the lengths she'd gone to to ensure otherwise, she wasn't over him at all?

Because if she was, she wouldn't have to spend every anniversary drunk out of her mind to avoid the memories, would she?

If she was, she wouldn't have found it so hard to drink out of those glasses.

If she was, she wouldn't be so afraid of mind-blowing sex, and she wouldn't only enter relationships with men who left her body completely unstirred.

If she was she wouldn't have felt so hurt at the thought Kit had just come here for sex.

'Do you want to know what I think, Lily?'

'No,' she said, her voice as croaky as if she hadn't used it for years.

'I think you're as over me as I am over you.'

She cleared her throat and tried to pull herself back on track. 'You can think what you like.'

'Can you honestly say you don't want me?'

No. 'Yes.'

'I don't believe you.'

'Too bad.'

'I want you.'

'Well, we can't always have what we want.'

'Can't we?' he murmured.

She set her jaw because whatever he wanted, whatever she might or might not want—and who knew the answer to that?—them sleeping together would be a disaster of titanic proportions and she had no intention of giving in. 'No.'

He moved closer, his gaze not letting her look away, and beneath its intensity she felt her resolve, her immunity to him begin to crumble. 'Are you sure about that?'

Her heart thundered. 'Quite sure.' And then at the predatory gleam in his eye, she added, 'What?'

'I've thought about you, you know.'

She shrugged as if she couldn't care less but inside she was beginning to shake. 'Have you?'

He nodded, his eyes glittering, and took a step forwards. 'A lot.'

'I haven't thought about you at all.'

'Really?'

She nodded. 'Really. Not once.'

'Don't you remember how it used to be?'

'I remember how it was in the end.'

'Coward.' He reached out and touched her hair while his gaze dipped to her mouth, and despite all her protests she shivered.

'Kiss me and you'll regret it,' she said, unfolding her arms and flexing and curling her fingers in warning, but that didn't seem to stop him.

He tilted his head and looked down at her, his eyes as

black as night and so full of intent and desire that she could barely breathe.

'That's a risk I'm prepared to take,' he muttered, and before she could even think of protesting he slid his hand round to the back of her neck then bent his head and captured her mouth with his.

CHAPTER FOUR

LILY TRIED TO keep her mouth closed and her eyes open, she really did, but the familiarity of Kit, the heat of his mouth, his body and his scent blew away her resistance like a dandelion on the wind, and within a second she found herself succumbing to the drugging desire that swept through her.

Her eyes fluttered shut and she moaned and his tongue thrust into her mouth with devilish intent. The heat and the spark she'd felt earlier and had ignored shot back with a rush and her knees went weak.

Any thought of pushing him away vanished. The fingers she'd been flexing in warning now clutched at his shirt to pull him closer because despite everything they'd been through, everything she'd tried to convince herself of over the years, she'd missed him. So damned much.

She could tell herself that she didn't want and didn't need that spark all she liked, but, goodness, she'd missed feeling like this. The heady, delirious rush of simple, hot desire, without any of the angst and anguish that had blighted the latter months of their marriage. She'd missed this kind of need, primitive, pure and fierce.

Just when she feared her legs were going to give way and she'd either fall into him or collapse into a heap on the floor Kit broke off the kiss and lifted his head.

'So is he or isn't he?' he asked roughly, his breathing all fast and ragged and his eyes glazed.

She stared up at him, her heart twisting and tugging, and she could feel herself falling under his spell just as she had the moment she'd looked into his eyes at the bottom of that ski slope in Italy.

The longer she looked up at him, the more her head began to swim with the emotions that she'd kept buried for so long and were now breaking free. Love, hate, joy, despair, desire.

And bewilderment, because had she spent the long lonely weeks, months, years since their divorce hoping for this? Hoping he'd come and find her? Had she been living a lie the whole of the last five years? And if she had, what did that make her? Nuts? Lucky? A hopeless case?

And what did all of this mean? Did Kit still feel something for her other than lust? Something more? Were there still feelings between them? Did they have a second chance?

Her mind teeming and her heart racing, Lily let the weight of emotion submerge the voice of reason bellowing in her head and warning her to be, oh, so very wary.

There'd be time for talk later, time for analysis and perhaps regret, perhaps hope. Right now, though, she just wanted him.

With excitement rushing through her and her pulse thundering, Lily took a deep, shaky breath, then said, 'Despite what I may have implied earlier Nick isn't my boyfriend, and he isn't going to be.'

Kit was wound so tight with tension and desire and the expectation of a slap across the face that for a moment he couldn't work out what Lily was saying.

And then, when his shell-shocked brain finally got round to working it out, couldn't quite believe it. Couldn't quite believe that the risk he'd taken had paid off.

Yet apparently, against all the odds, it had, because here she was, not moving, not lifting her hand to slap him. In fact her eyes were shining, her chest was heaving and she was giving him the kind of look they'd shared at the beginning of their relationship, the one that was filled with heat and need and desperation and had always made his head spin.

That acting on what was clearly going through both their minds wasn't a good idea didn't seem to matter. That there was so much between them and starting something up again would only make things worse and set them back years seemed an irrelevance.

Kit was drowning beneath a wave of desire that had been absent for so long and lust was hammering through him so strong and hot that it drugged his senses, wiped out his reason and everything but the thought that he needed this and he needed Lily. With a desperation and hunger that was eating him up. And it was the same for her too judging by the way she'd just kissed him back.

With one quick move, before she had time to rethink the wisdom of her choice, Kit had her back in his arms and was then twisting her round away from the door and backing her up against the hall wall. The feel of her, the heat of her blasted into him and a bolt of sheer desire powered through him.

He planted his hands on either side of her head while she threw her arms around his neck and then their mouths met, tongues tangled and his mind went blank.

He'd never met anyone who kissed as Lily did, who threw themselves into it with everything they had and everything they felt. Kissing her had always been intoxicating and it was no different now. It was familiar and hot and made him burn.

As did the little moans coming from the back of her throat and the way she was melting against him.

Moving his hand, he buried it in her hair and angled her head so he could kiss her deeper, harder, and she responded with equal need.

Breaking for breath several long, hot minutes later, Kit pulled back and stared down into her eyes. 'Are you sure about this?' he muttered.

'No,' she said dazedly, her breathing all ragged and harsh. 'Are you?'

'Hell, no.'

'Then what are we doing? What is this?'

'Who knows?' he said, sliding his hand round to her jaw and stroking his thumb over her lower lip. 'Irresistible chemistry. Undeniable attraction. A disaster, probably.'

'You could be right.'

'Want to stop?' It might kill him but if she was having second thoughts he couldn't blame her.

'Don't you dare.'

She pulled his head back down to hers and started kissing him again. And then things switched up a gear because she was making sounds—familiar, encouraging sounds—that he hadn't heard for years, and tugging at his clothes, reaching beneath his coat, pulling his shirt from the waistband of his jeans and pushing it up.

He could feel her impatience, but it wasn't a patch on his, and as she put her hands on the bare skin of his back it sent such a shot of desire through him that Kit couldn't wait any longer.

Breaking the kiss, both of them breathing hard, Kit lowered his hands to her thighs, slid her dress up and wrenched her knickers down, feeling as he did so how wet, how ready for him she was. He released her for a moment so that she could kick them off while he grappled with his belt. Which, with shaking hands, was frustratingly difficult.

'Let me,' Lily muttered, brushing his hands aside, unbuckling his belt and then making swift work of the buttons of his jeans.

As she slipped a hand inside his shorts and caressed the

rock-hard, aching length of him he groaned and nearly exploded right there and then.

'Enough,' he muttered, removing her hand and planting it on his neck.

'Hurry,' she said with an urgency that nearly obliterated his control.

'Hold on to me.'

She did, wrapping her arms round his neck and her legs round his waist as he lifted her, pressed her back against the wall for support, and with relief, desire and heat rushing through him he drove into her.

At the warm, wet feel of her he let out a groan of pleasure, relief and who knew what else.

Lily moaned, dropped her head back but, honestly, he was too far gone to notice much what she was doing. All he could feel, and all he could think, was that he was in absolute heaven.

Then she moved and as heaven came that little bit closer Kit realised he was in deep trouble. Because he wanted to go slow, savour the moment, make sure that she was with him every step of the way, but it had been so long, so incredibly long, and if she didn't hold still he'd lose what little control he had left.

'Stop moving,' he said roughly, his fingers digging into her thighs in an effort to hold her still.

'I can't help it,' she whimpered.

As he gritted his teeth against the pressure she held on to him tighter, pressed herself closer. He could hear her breathing go haywire, could feel her tight around him, hear those little pants and he began to spin out of control.

'Stop it now, Lily.'

'No, it feels too good.'

She tilted her hips, pulled him in deeper and that triggered a primitive need in him he couldn't begin to comprehend, let alone control. His head swam with the urge to take, to possess, to reclaim. His heart thundered and inside him there was simply too much urgency. Too much build-up. Too much everything, and his resistance collapsed beneath the sheer force of it.

His control now history, instinct took over and, with the sound of Lily's whimpers and sobbing moans in his ear, he started blindly thrusting in and out of her, faster and harder, unable to stop or even slow down.

And just when the tightness gripping his lower body became unbearable, just when he thought he was about to implode beneath the pressure, or die from the intensity of the pleasure, he lost it.

With a great groan he erupted inside her, pulsating and spilling into her for what felt like for ever.

As hot sexual encounters went that one hadn't quite delivered on its promise, thought Lily, her heart thumping, her breathing skittery and her body twitching and aching with unfulfilled desire while Kit collapsed against her.

But that was OK. She didn't have to be up until seven and she had plenty of experience at recovering after burning the candle at both ends. Later she had a ten-hour plane ride during which she could catch up on sleep, and Kit spending the rest of the night making it up to her would be well worth any fatigue she suffered.

'I'm sorry,' Kit muttered, his voice muffled against her neck.

'Don't worry about it,' she said softly, stroking the back of his neck and smiling at the thought of what was to come.

'How could I not worry about it? That hasn't happened to me since I was sixteen. I didn't even take my coat off.'

A sense of pride surged up inside her at the memory of how keen he'd been. 'Anyone would think it's been a while.'

'Anyone would be right.'

'Really? How long?' Surely it couldn't rival the eighteen-month drought she'd had.

Not that she particularly wanted to think of him with a string of girlfriends, but the undeniable fact was that he was gorgeous, about to enter some rich list or another and, according to the gossip columns that she definitely didn't read, single. A man like Kit wouldn't lack company.

He sighed and her skin tingled beneath the warmth of his breath. 'Five years.'

Lily stopped stroking his neck, frozen with astonishment. 'What?'

'Don't make me repeat it.'

'You haven't had sex for five years?'

'Not since our divorce.'

'Truly?'

He grimaced. 'You think it's something I'd make up?'

It wasn't. Who would?

And because it wasn't and because of what it meant Lily felt instantly sick. Her blood went cold and her body went numb and her throat went tight.

Not because she'd weakened and let herself fall under Kit's spell. And not because she was feeling twitchy with need and could feel him still hard inside her.

No. What was making her want to throw up, what was making her suddenly all shivery and achy and what was making her suddenly desperate to get him the hell out of her body and her house was the realisation that the last person he had had sex with before her just now must have been the woman he'd picked up at some work do while their marriage lay in ruins.

The knowledge triggered a deluge of memories. The devastation she'd felt when he'd told her what had happened. The excoriating hurt and agonising sense of betrayal. And then the pain and the disillusionment and the realisation that they really were over.

As the memories hit furious and fast she could feel a great wave of emotion begin to roll towards her, could feel herself about to break apart and she had to swallow hard to free her throat of the lump that had lodged there.

Unwinding her legs from around his waist, she shifted herself off him just as fast as she could. How could she have been so stupid? How could she have thrown away five years of protecting herself with such abandon? She'd fallen back into Kit's arms without a care for herself. What the hell had she been thinking? How could she have resisted so little? How could she ever have imagined that they might be able to make another go of things? How could she have even wanted to?

Unable to look at him because God knew what he'd see in her eyes or on her face, she pulled her dress down and then used her fingers to smooth her tangled hair.

'Lily?' asked Kit, the concern in his voice showing that he'd sensed something had changed.

'What?' she said blankly, casting her gaze around the floor for her knickers and dimly aware that he was fixing his clothing and tucking his shirt into his jeans.

'Are you all right?'

She bent down and swiped them up. 'I'm fine.'

As she straightened he reached out to touch her face and she recoiled as if he'd struck her. Frowning, he pulled back and stared at her. 'What's wrong?'

'I think you'd better go.'

She needed space. Time. Privacy to examine the wounds, the scars of which had just been ripped off.

'Not until you tell me what's the matter.'

'Nothing's the matter,' she said flatly. 'You got what you wanted. Now go.'

He blanched at the bite of her tone. 'I'm sorry I couldn't wait.'

As if that was what was upsetting her. 'Forget it.'

'No.'

'Look, I was wrong,' she said, bracing herself and looking up at him. 'This was a mistake. An awful mistake that should never have happened and now I'd really like it if you went. Please.'

He must have heard the finality in her voice, must have sensed her weariness or something else, because for a long time he just looked at her. Then he nodded. 'OK, fine,' he said with a frown. 'I'll call you in the morning.'

And with that, he turned on his heel, opened the door and left.

Lily was avoiding him. That was the only explanation for it.

Kit sat at his desk in his office in the penthouse apartment of his London flagship hotel and the place he called home, and glowered at his phone, which might have been broken for all the use it had been so far.

All morning he'd been trying to get hold of her, but infuriatingly her home landline just rang and rang before the answer machine eventually kicked in, and her mobile went straight to voicemail. The brief email he'd fired off asking her to call him had also gone annoyingly unanswered.

Rubbing a hand along his jaw, Kit reflected back to the way things had ended last night and thought he could sort of understand why Lily might not want to speak to him. He'd had the time of his life and she hadn't. She must have been disappointed. Frustrated. Exhausted. It had sounded as if she'd had a busy night even before he'd shown up, and what with such an anticlimax perhaps everything had simply got too much.

In his albeit out-of-date experience, Lily's way of dealing with an emotional overload had always been to shut down, so actually the way she'd responded hadn't been all that unusual.

Nor had the way he'd responded to her. As he'd done

so often in the past, he'd given her the space he thought she needed and left her to it, even though he hadn't really wanted to.

But that wasn't the right way to play it. With hindsight it probably never had been. It was entirely possible that the fact that she'd always withdrawn whenever things had got too heavy going and he'd basically let her, under the guise of giving her space, was how things had got so bad so quickly between them.

He should have been firmer all those years ago and insisted that they face things together, however hard. Lily had been right when she'd said that they'd neither talked nor listened; they hadn't.

Well, whatever had happened in the past, things were going to be different now, he thought, clicking on his inbox for the dozenth time in as many minutes to see if she'd replied. Now he was going to insist on both talking and listening, and that was why her going off grid was so frustrating.

Because apart from deciding that their inability to communicate needed to be fixed, over the course of the night he'd been struck by a truckload of realisations, reached a dozen new conclusions and had come up with a whole load of questions, some of which he wouldn't mind putting to her.

Such as, what had Lily meant by saying that if he'd asked she might have given him an apology for what she'd done? Why had she let him think that she was going out with someone when she wasn't? And why the abrupt change in her demeanour in the minutes before he left? One minute she'd been all warm and soft and then next she'd gone all cold and frigid on him, and he wanted to know why.

Mainly, though, he'd realised that whatever he felt for her, and whatever she felt for him, they weren't over. Not by a long shot.

Setting his jaw, Kit reached for the phone again and was

about to hit the redial button when he paused as a thought occurred to him. Despite it being a public holiday, maybe Lily was at work. Maybe that was why there was no answer from home. Maybe she was on the tube and her mobile out of range of a signal. Maybe she was in a meeting. It could be that she wasn't avoiding him. Merely busy.

Filling with renewed resolve, he looked up her company's details then punched the number into his phone and sat back to wait while it rang. His stomach churned and his mouth went dry, but that was probably down to the fact that it had been a while since his last coffee and he'd been too preoccupied to bother with breakfast.

'MMS, good morning.'

'Zoe?' he said, recognising the voice of his former sister-in-law.

'Yes. How can I help?'

'It's Kit.'

There was a long silence. Then a faint, 'Oh.'

'How are you?'

'Fine. Yes. Good… Kind of surprised to hear from you, to be honest.'

'It's been a while.'

'You can say that again. How are you?'

'Fine. Happy New Year.'

'You too.' She paused. 'So…were you after Lily?'

'Is she there?'

'No. But then I'm at home. The office is closed today so your call was diverted to my mobile.'

'Right.' He frowned. That blew his theory that Lily was at work out of the water. Of course she wasn't. Who was? It was New Year's Day. So was she avoiding him after all?

'Is there a problem or something?' asked Zoe and he snapped back to the conversation.

'She's not answering either of her phones or replying to emails.'

'No, well, she wouldn't be.'

'Why not?'

'Because she's on a plane.'

Kit frowned, a bit taken aback. A plane? She hadn't mentioned anything about going away. Not that she'd been under any obligation to, but still… 'When will she be back?'

'Not for a couple of weeks.'

A couple of weeks? He wasn't sure he could wait that long. Patience had never been his strong point—probably one more contributory factor to the breakdown of their marriage—and right now it was wearing increasingly thin.

'Right. I see,' he said, switching to his agenda with a couple of clicks and seeing that there wasn't anything that couldn't be moved or dealt with by someone else for a couple of weeks. 'Where is she?'

'I can't tell you that.'

'Why not?'

'Well, for one thing, she's on a job and the work she's doing requires a certain degree of anonymity and a low profile.'

'And for another?'

'And for another I don't think she'd thank me if I told you where she was. Do you really think she wants to see you after everything?'

Kit set his jaw and took a deep breath. 'She was happy enough to see me last night.' Which was a slight stretch of the truth, but desperate times called for desperate measures.

There was a pause. 'Last night?'

'We spent it together.'

'Really?'

'Part of it.'

He heard Zoe blowing out a breath. 'Jeez.'

'I need to talk to her, Zoe.'

'She'll be back in a couple of weeks. You can talk to her then.'

'I can't wait that long.'

'After five years, you can't wait two weeks?'

'No.'

'Why not?'

'I'm not sure.'

'Do you still love her?'

Kit felt the totally unexpected question hit him like a punch to the chest.

Did he?

He'd spent the last five years thinking he didn't, but who knew? Seeing her again last night had thrown everything he'd always assumed about their relationship and his life for the last five years into question, so how he felt about Lily or anything for that matter was now up in the air.

The only thing he *was* sure about was that they weren't done. Quite apart from all the questions he had for her, he hadn't apologised for what he'd done all those years ago and for basically blaming her for it. He hadn't told her of the guilt he carried or asked her for her forgiveness, and the need to put all of this right burned inside him like a hot coal.

Last night had opened doors he'd never imagined would ever open again, and now—even if they were only slightly ajar—he wasn't about to let them close. Not only did he seek redemption, he also had the feeling that he was hovering on the brink of a second chance with Lily here, and even though it had never crossed his mind before, had never been something he'd thought he wanted, he now realised he wanted it more than anything, and if that didn't tell him that he still had feelings for her he didn't know what would.

'I don't know,' he said, erring on the side of caution because how he felt about Lily still needed further analysis. 'Maybe. Maybe not. Either way, there are things we need to figure out. Please, Zoe.'

There was another long silence while Zoe presumably

weighed up the pros and cons of telling him and he held his breath.

'Oh, OK,' she said eventually and Kit felt the tension drain from his shoulders. 'But look, she really is working so you can't go barging in there right now.'

'When, then?'

'She finishes next Sunday. Afterwards she's staying on for a few days' holiday until the following Saturday.'

He rubbed a hand along his jaw while his brain raced. He could wait a week, couldn't he? It would give him time to think. Plan. Delegate. Figure out exactly what he wanted to say and how he was going to say it, and how he was going to persuade her to give them the second chance he thought they had. And actually, neutral territory, without any association to the past, might be just the thing.

'Fine,' he said, 'I'll wait. You have my word.'

'Hmm,' said Zoe, sounding as though she didn't think his word counted for much.

'Where is she, Zoe?' he said, ignoring the sting of his ex-sister-in-law's scepticism because right now he had more important things to focus on.

'On her way to the Indian Ocean. Santa Teresa Island. She's staying at the Coral Bay Lodge.'

'Thank you.'

'Look, Kit, Lily hasn't had a holiday in years. She's really looking forward to it. It took her ages to get over you. Tell me I'm not going to regret having told you where she's going.'

'You won't regret it.'

He'd make sure of it.

CHAPTER FIVE

As JOBS WENT, this one hadn't exactly been a hardship, thought Lily, settling on her sun lounger and preparing herself to test the customer service levels of the beach-bar staff, although this time for her own personal pleasure.

Some were, some weren't. That was the way it went, and had gone, right from the start. MMS had started off offering customer satisfaction surveys before expanding to include services such as employee performance analysis, consumer demographic studies and bespoke training programmes, all in the name of driving service excellence. Their clients came in all shapes and sizes and temperaments.

This particular—easy—client had been with them since their inception and had grown with similar speed. Somehow, as the by-product of a much larger deal they'd ended up with a portfolio of assets that included the island of Santa Teresa. They'd offloaded the assets they didn't want, but had decided to keep Santa Teresa with its once five-star luxury resort to see what they could do with it. They'd hired MMS to conduct a thorough analysis of how to turn the business around on the consumer side of things.

Normally MMS contracted the fieldwork out. In their business anonymity was key, and employing a small band of discreet, trustworthy, reliable freelancers to go wherever they were needed allowed Lily to concentrate on the marketing, sales and client side of the business and Zoe to focus on the numbers and data analysis.

On this occasion, however, the woman they'd hired to spend a week assessing the performance of staff and the overall consumer experience at the Coral Bay Lodge had slipped on ice and broken her ankle over Christmas and couldn't fly. At such short notice, especially over the holiday season, they hadn't been able to get anyone else so Lily had taken on the job.

Actually, she'd been heartily grateful for the distraction. January in London was typically on the quiet side and if she'd been there twiddling her thumbs she'd have had hours in which to dwell on everything that had happened on New Year's Eve. Instead she'd been so busy working, concentrating on the details and reporting back to Zoe with her findings that she hadn't given Kit a moment's thought.

Well, *hardly* a moment's thought, she amended, picking up the cocktail menu and wondering whether five in the afternoon was too early for a sundowner.

He *had* slipped into her head on the odd unguarded occasion, but whenever he did hot on the heels of it came the instant realisation of just what a bad idea Sunday night had been, how much what he'd done still hurt and how stupid and deluded she'd been to even imagine that him showing up on her doorstep might mean anything other than the need to scratch an itch.

Thank goodness the sex had been lousy or she'd be in serious trouble, she reflected, glancing down the long list of cocktails. If it had been as mind-blowing as she knew it could be, she'd now undoubtedly be wondering what she'd been missing all these years. What she'd been thinking when she'd decided to pursue relationships with men who didn't affect her pulse rate.

She might also well be letting good sex get in the way of good judgement and telling herself that maybe she'd overreacted on Sunday night. She might be thinking that perhaps everything that had gone on between them before was now water under the bridge and why on earth shouldn't they try again?

Despite the heat of the day Lily felt a shiver run down her spine. Wow, what a lucky escape she'd had.

And continued to have because thankfully since the day following the night before she hadn't heard from Kit. Oh, that Monday he'd called. Repeatedly. At least, she assumed it had been him; she didn't have his number in her phone, but he'd said he would, and she couldn't think of anyone else whose number her phone didn't recognise who would keep popping up with such persistence.

By the time the tube to Heathrow had emerged above ground, she'd seen she had half a dozen missed calls but, feeling too tired and too emotionally on edge to deal with the conversation she could imagine he'd want to have, she'd switched her phone off.

She'd switched it on twelve hours later and braced herself for more missed calls, but they seemed to have dried up. Which she was delighted by. Really, she was.

Smiling up at the waiter who'd materialised beneath her thatch umbrella as if able to read her mind, Lily ordered a margarita. It wasn't too early and, besides, so what if it was? This was the first holiday she'd had in two years, and she planned to enjoy it.

After all, how could she not? she thought, lying back as the waiter smoothly retreated, putting her sunglasses on and closing her eyes with a deep sigh of satisfaction.

The endless azure-blue sky had been unblemished by cloud for the entire last week and the temperature was on average a perfect twenty-eight degrees. She'd downloaded a dozen books to read and there were miles of white sandy beaches to stroll along should she want the exercise. Ditto the sea, which was clear and turquoise and incredibly inviting. And what with the fabulous restaurant and beach bar she wasn't planning on moving for the entire week.

Lily was on the point of dropping off when the quick tensing of her muscles and the sudden jump in her heart rate alerted her to the fact that someone was standing over her.

The waiter with her cocktail, she thought delightedly, levering herself up, whipping off her sunglasses and opening her eyes.

And nearly passing out with shock at the sight of Kit looming over her, blocking out the sun and holding what looked like her drink.

Oh, no, she thought, her heart plummeting as she stared up at him. There went her plans to relax.

'Hello, Lily,' he said casually, his deep voice sending goosebumps scattering all over her skin.

'Hello, Kit,' she replied, adding a cool smile to show that she could do casual too.

Acting like an automaton, she sat up, swung her legs round and reached for the sarong she'd dropped on the neighbouring sun lounger. With an odd feeling of calm she stood up and wrapped it round her, covering up the bikini that she'd thought modest when she'd put it on this morning but right now felt like the skimpiest thing she'd ever worn.

She tied the ends of the sarong between her breasts and took a moment to arrange her thoughts. Thoughts that actually weren't in nearly as much disarray as they ought to have been, she had to acknowledge. Because the strange thing was in all honesty she wasn't all that surprised to see him. Kit had always been proactive, and what with the way things had been left between them and the way she'd ignored his calls she should have guessed that he wouldn't have let it lie. In fact, she should have realised something was afoot when the calls had stopped.

'Yours, I believe.' He held out her drink.

Lily took it, ensuring that their fingers didn't accidentally brush. 'Thank you,' she said. 'The hotel business not doing too well these days, darling? Having to moonlight as a waiter?'

Kit shot her a smile that despite her intention to stay cool and unruffled made her hot and bothered in a way that had nothing to do with the afternoon heat. 'The hotel business is doing great. And as I was on my way over anyway I thought I'd save him the trip.'

Lily lifted the glass to her lips, swallowed down a massive gulp and winced as the tequila shot down her throat and hit her stomach. 'So thoughtful.'

'I can be.'

She licked the salt from her lips and felt a sharp stab of satisfaction when his gaze dropped to her mouth for a second. 'This is beginning to become a bit of a habit,' she said.

'What is?'

'You showing up unexpectedly.'

'I might be on holiday.'

Yeah, right. 'Are you?'

'Yes.'

'My, what a coincidence.'

'Isn't it just? Do you mind if I join you?'

Yes. 'Not at all,' she said, waving a hand in the direction of the sun lounger to her right as she sat down. 'Be my guest.'

Kit took off his sunglasses, folded them and hooked one arm over the V of his T-shirt. Then he sat down and leaned forwards, resting his elbows on his knees.

As his eyes met hers Lily felt herself beginning to lose track of things, as she often did when she looked into his eyes, and she wished he'd kept his sunglasses on. Instead she put her own back on, and waited.

'I was told you were staying at the Coral Bay Lodge,' said Kit.

'Who by?'

'Zoe.'

Of course. No one else apart from the client knew she was in this part of the world. But what the hell did Zoe think she was doing? Normally her sister was the soul of discretion, so what had happened? How could she ever have thought that Lily would want to see Kit? How had he ever persuaded her to release the details? Had he said something about what had happened between them on New Year's Eve, and Zoe, in her current state of ecstatic happiness and filled with the resultant determination for everyone else to feel the same, was under some warped misconception that she was facilitating a reconciliation?

Whatever the reason, Lily thought darkly, she and her sister would be having words just as soon she was free to call. 'When did you speak to her?'

'New Year's Day.'

A week ago. 'Right. Why?'

'I rang you, but you didn't pick up.'

'I was travelling.'

'You didn't return my calls.'

'I didn't know it was you.'

He arched a sceptical eyebrow. 'Didn't you?'

'You should have left a message.'

'Would you have called me back if I had?'

'Of course.'

'Sure about that? Because I don't remember getting a reply to my email.'

Lily smiled and shrugged nonchalantly. 'Well, I guess we'll never know, will we?'

'I guess not.'

'So were you worried about me, Kit? Ah, that's sweet.'

'I wasn't worried in the slightest,' he said easily. 'I merely wanted to talk to you. This seemed to be the only way of achieving that.'

'I'm flattered.'

'You should be. You were tricky to track down.'

'I moved hotels.'

'You moved islands.'

Lily took another gulp of her margarita. 'Yes, well, these islands are small. My hanging around on Santa Teresa once my work was done might have looked a bit odd.'

'It took me longer than I'd expected to find you.'

'Are you after an apology?'

'Would I get one?'

'Not this time.'

Kit grinned that heart-fluttering grin of his and her stomach flipped in a way she didn't like at all. 'Didn't think so,' he murmured.

'Couldn't you have waited until I got back? I haven't had a holiday in years.'

'Patience isn't one of my strong points.'

'No.' She paused and then gave it one last futile, she suspected, shot. 'Is there anything at all I can do to make you go away?'

'Not a thing.'

No, she hadn't thought so. Lily sighed and resigned herself to the inevitable. 'OK, fine. You win. But I'm not dressed for a chat.' She certainly wasn't ready.

He ran his gaze over her, so slowly and thoroughly that she felt as if he'd stripped her bare. 'You look fine to me,' he said, a little hoarsely she thought, 'but perhaps you're right. Maybe this isn't the time or the place.'

Never and nowhere would be the right time and place in her opinion, but what could she do? On an island this size she'd never be able to avoid him, and hopping on the next available boat to the mainland wasn't the answer because not only was running away immature, as Kit had just proved, he'd simply come in search of her.

Anyway, it would probably be fine. All they were going to do was talk, and talking never killed anyone, did it?

Besides, on one of the *extremely* rare occasions that Kit had flitted into her head over the last week she'd reflected that she'd been wrong when on her doorstep a week ago she'd told him they'd never been able to talk. Communication between the two of them had always been fine when there wasn't much of import to communicate. The problems had only arisen when the stakes had been stratospheric, when emotions had run high and they'd felt exposed and vulnerable. It was then that they'd both gone into hiding and communication had become a four-letter word.

Tonight there wouldn't be anything at stake. Kit might make her feel a bit on edge, and, God, he looked mouth-wateringly, spine-tinglingly hot in the white polo shirt, khaki shorts combination he was currently wearing, but she wasn't emotionally involved. Not now.

And, actually, if he wanted to rake through the ashes of their relationship, that was fine with her because there were things she needed to tell him. Things she'd come to realise over the last five years. Things that she wanted to get off her chest and he ought to know.

She was much stronger than she'd been all those years ago, and with the exception of the wobble she'd had on New Year's Eve, which had merely been down to shock anyway, he didn't have the ability to hurt her any more.

Therefore, if she was well prepared and stayed focused conversation with Kit would be fine. Cathartic even. 'Shall we have dinner?'

'The restaurant?'

Of course the restaurant; no way was she inviting him to her villa for room service. 'Why not?'

'Eight o'clock?'

Three hours in which to decide her strategy? Three hours in which to don her suit of armour? Or, despite her brave thoughts just now, three hours in which to get completely and utterly hammered? Whichever route she chose to take three hours was perfect.

Draining the rest of her margarita and ignoring the small bundle of nerves beginning to twist her stomach, Lily nodded coolly. 'Eight o'clock it is.'

The terrace where dining took place was everything that could be expected of a luxury four-figure-a-night five-star resort on an island off the coast of Mozambique. Lanterns sat on the edge of the decking, the candles within flickering in the twilight. Tables set with starched white tablecloths, silver cutlery and fine crystal dotted the terrace and the beach. Soft, sultry music drifted from behind the bar into the warm evening air.

Nature lent quite a hand to the feeling of sensuality too. The sea rushed up the sand with a gentle swish and then rolled back. The heady scent of lady of the night drifted through the warm evening air. The palm trees that surrounded the restaurant rustled in the breeze and cicadas chirped in the undergrowth.

Utterly oblivious to the considerable charms of the establishment, however, was Kit, who was standing at the bar and frowning down at his beer as he experienced a rare yet all-consuming moment of self-doubt.

Heading over here had seemed such a good idea last week when he'd put his plans into place. Fired up on adrenalin and the thrill of the chase, and practically burning up with the idea of a second chance with Lily, he'd had his secretary make the travel arrangements while he'd issued instructions to his management team. He'd found himself looking forward to seeing her again and the challenges he knew he could expect. He'd been looking forward to getting everything off his chest and persuading her to give them another shot. More than looking forward to it, if he was being honest.

But now he was here, now he'd seen her clear hostility towards him—which she'd been less successful at hiding than she probably thought—it struck him that maybe he'd been a bit reckless. And maybe he wasn't being very fair.

OK, so he wanted to talk things through and offload, but perhaps Lily didn't. Who was he to insist they rake up the past when, considering the boyfriends she'd mentioned, she'd evidently moved on in a way that he didn't think he had?

By turning up out of the blue like this and demanding they talk he'd put her in an impossible position. He'd probably shot her intentions to relax and enjoy her holiday to pieces. Given what he knew of her he wouldn't be all that surprised if she'd hopped on a boat to the mainland to catch the next flight home. Or at the very least hotfooted it to one of the other islands that made up the archipelago in an effort to put some distance between them and resume her holiday in peace.

Either one of which was looking increasingly likely, he thought, glancing at his watch, because it was now quarter past eight and Lily was never late.

Beating back the disappointment beginning to sweep through him, Kit swallowed hard and forced himself to focus on practicalities. If she wasn't late, if she had gone, what would he do next? Go after her again and this time lock her up or something to make flight impossible? Leave her in peace until they got home? Or give up altogether?

As his stomach began to churn Kit exhaled slowly and told himself to calm down. He'd give her another fifteen minutes, then he'd put in a call, and, depending on whether or how she answered, would take things from there.

Thirty seconds later, however, the doubt over whether or not she'd left and what he'd do about it vanished because despite having his back to the entrance to the bar he knew Lily was there. He could feel it in the way his muscles tensed with awareness, the prickling of his skin, the overwhelming sense of relief that flooded through him.

Deliberately slowly he set down his beer, turned round, and at the sight of her his heart stopped. For a moment he felt winded. Blinded. Stunned. She was wearing a simple floaty black dress and sparkly flip-flops, and she was clutching a small black bag. Her neck was bare but big silvery hooped earrings hung from her earlobes.

Her dress wasn't particularly revealing or overly clingy, yet something about her made his mouth go dry. It was as if she were sort of glowing from the inside out. Her dark hair shone in the soft light of the bar and her eyes gleamed and her mouth was curved into a barely there smile that had his pulse racing.

She looked… He racked his brains for a moment to find the right word. Serene. That was it. She looked serene.

While he felt anything but.

With his heart beating double time Kit watched as she walked over to him and for the first time in years felt a stab of panic because he didn't know whether to kiss her mouth, her cheek, shake her hand or do nothing.

His indecision was as terrifying as the decision he had to make, and his palms went damp in a way that had nothing to do with the condensation that he'd felt on his beer glass.

With every step she took his head swam just that little bit more, until she stopped right in front of him and, thank goodness, took the decision out of his hands by reaching up and planting a soft, light kiss on his cheek.

Then she stepped back and smiled up at him, presumably completely unaware of how she was affecting him.

'You look nice,' she said, giving him a quick once-over that had heat shooting through him.

'You look beautiful,' he replied, once he'd managed to clear his head of her scent and unglue his tongue from the roof of his mouth.

'Thank you.'

He cleared his throat. 'I booked a table.'

'Great.'

'Would you like a drink before we sit down?'

'Would you?'

'If you would.'

'I don't mind.'

Feeling as if a swarm of bees had invaded his body, Kit swallowed hard. For crying out loud, this was absurd. He was thirty-two. He ran a global multimillion-pound business. He was known for being decisive, intuitive and utterly ruthless when the situation called for it. Yet here he was, being rendered practically tongue-tied by the prospect of an evening with his ex-wife. His totally calm and in control ex-wife. Who was expecting not a drooling idiot of a dining companion, but a possibly difficult conversation that he'd insisted upon.

Telling himself he really had to get a grip, with superhuman effort Kit pulled himself together. 'Let's just go straight to the table, shall we?' he muttered, taking her hand and practically marching her across the bar and out onto the sand.

CHAPTER SIX

THIS WASN'T A DATE. This wasn't a date. This wasn't a date.

As she followed Kit to the table that sat at the water's edge and was set for two Lily tried to concentrate on the mantra rolling around her head and not on the electricity that emanated from the connection of her hand with his and was zapping through her, but it was proving no more helpful now than it had when she'd been getting ready.

After going back to her room earlier this afternoon and taking a cold shower, which hadn't done much to obliterate the hundred or so grasshoppers that had seemed to have taken up residence in her stomach at the thought of the date—no, *dinner*—with Kit, she'd decided that while donning armour was a must, mainlining tequila probably wasn't the way to handle the evening. She was in a jittery enough state as it was and with alcohol loosening her already iffy inhibitions who knew what might happen?

Once she'd made that pleasingly mature decision, she'd called her sister and after that, well, she hadn't known what to think about anything.

As she'd dialled the number she'd been planning to tear a strip off Zoe for revealing her whereabouts to Kit of all people. She'd been going to say she understood that her sister was at a heightened level of happiness at the moment, but that she had to realise that not everyone was in search of the same, and that *she* certainly wasn't looking for it with Kit. She'd even been prepared to counter-argue the excuse of Kit's powers of persuasion she was sure Zoe was going to give.

What she hadn't been prepared for, however, was her sister's declaration that she thought Kit still had feelings for her, that he'd said he might still love her and that *that* was why she'd told him where she was. To give them the opportunity to see whether they had a second chance. Or something.

In something of a daze Lily had hung up, and it was then that she'd descended into the kind of emotional turmoil she'd spent so long avoiding, her head teeming with questions such as 'Could he?' 'Did he?' and her heart beginning to swell with what she had the awful suspicion might be hope.

Which made such a mockery of everything she'd spent the last five years trying to convince herself of that it was no wonder she'd worked herself up into such a state. For the best part of the next couple of hours she'd paced up and down her room wondering whether her sister had got it right and then trying to figure out that if she had, what she— Lily—wanted, if anything, and what, if anything, she felt.

Before she knew it it was half past seven and she still hadn't dried her hair. Bafflingly none the wiser about how she felt about any of it, she'd put it to the back of her mind while she got ready, and there it had stayed until she'd seen him standing at the bar, nursing his beer and looking so familiar and so gorgeous that her heart had turned over and her brain had turned to jelly and she couldn't think about anything at all.

So she'd schooled her features into a neutral arrangement that she hoped masked the craziness that was going on inside her head, had taken a deep, steadying breath and told herself to remember what dinner was about.

But, heavens, it was difficult to focus when her head

was filled with the look on Kit's face when he'd turned and seen her. She didn't think she was wearing anything particularly astonishing but from the heat in his eyes she felt as if she were the most beautiful woman he'd ever seen. Perhaps on the planet.

It was even harder to concentrate on the reason they were here when everything about the place, from the lighting to the music and even the positioning of the tables, screamed intimacy, privacy and romance.

They reached their table at the same time as a waiter, who pulled out Lily's chair, waited for her to sit down and then did the same for Kit opposite. He handed them each a menu, took their order for aperitifs and then melted away.

Glancing down at the list of dishes, each of which sounded more mouth-watering than the previous, Lily swiftly made her choice. As did Kit, judging by the way he put the menu down with a brief nod and sat back.

Her eyes met his, their gazes locked and as the seconds ticked by she became achingly aware of the beating of her heart, the sound of her breathing, of every inch of her body come to think of it. The connection between them was as strong as ever, the attraction undeniable, and the tension, the heat and the anticipation still simmered.

'I'm glad you're here,' said Kit eventually, the faint surprise in his voice as much as his words snapping her out of her reverie.

Lily swallowed hard and gave herself a quick mental shake. She had to get a grip. She really did if she was going to make it through dinner. 'What, here on the island?' she asked, which she didn't think made much sense. 'Or here at this table?' Which did.

'Here with me. Now.'

'Why wouldn't I be?'

'It had crossed my mind that you might have used the afternoon to run away.'

Ah, he knew her so well. 'It crossed mine too,' she said with a small smile, 'but then I figured what would that have achieved? Avoidance isn't the way to deal with any of this.'

Kit leaned back and looked at her, a thoughtful expression flickering across his face in the twilight. 'What is?'

She gave a little shrug. 'I'm not sure. Honesty maybe?'

'Honesty works for me.'

He glanced up and smiled his thanks at the waiter who'd set a glass of champagne in front of her and was now doing the same with his beer for him and her breath caught. Goodness, his smile really was something else. She'd been on the receiving end of it so many times but it had never failed to affect her. Still didn't, it seemed, because the waiter was looking down at her expectantly as apparently it was time to order and she couldn't for the life of her remember what she'd chosen.

Indicating that Kit should go first with a wave of her hand, Lily picked up the menu and while he ordered lobster followed by tilapia she found with relief her starter of prawns and main of curried sea bass.

'I'm sorry about New Year's Eve,' said Kit once the waiter had disappeared with their order and they were once again alone.

'New Year's Eve?' echoed Lily, her eyebrows lifting a little. 'Why? What is there to be sorry about?'

'What isn't there to be sorry about?' he muttered, shifting in his chair as if suddenly finding it uncomfortable. 'I turned up out of the blue, virtually forced you to let me in and then behaved like a crazed hormonal out-of-control teenager.'

'Oh, right,' she said, feeling herself flush at the memory of how out of control they'd both been. How reckless and deluded *she'd* been. 'Well, consider your apology accepted.'

'Thanks.'

'You're welcome.'

See, they could be perfectly civilised about this, she thought, taking a sip of champagne, which was cold and dry and utterly delicious. Even if she was a total mess inside.

'I wasn't surprised you threw me out what with the… ah…way things went,' he said and went a little red.

She stared at him for a second and then put her glass down. 'You think I threw you out because I was cross I hadn't, well, you know…?' Neither of them was usually such a prude about these things, but then normally they didn't discuss them in public. At least she didn't.

Now it was he who raised his eyebrows. 'Didn't you?'

'Of course not.'

'Then what happened?'

'When you told me that you hadn't had sex for five years it occurred to me that the last woman you'd slept with was, well, you know…' She braced herself, then in the spirit of the honesty she'd just claimed she believed was the way forwards, said, 'Her.'

Kit frowned. 'I see.'

'It freaked me out. Brought back a time I've spent five years trying to forget.'

He rubbed a hand over his face. 'Of course. I'm sorry.'

'I realise now that I might have overreacted a bit, but in my defence it had been quite an emotionally stressful night, even before you turned up.' She shrugged and shot him a faint smile. 'Anyway, it's not your fault.'

'Isn't it?' he asked, his face dark and his eyes glittering in the twilight. 'Isn't everything?'

And there it was. The moment she could either agree that it was and they'd stay where they were, with Kit in all likelihood heading home and out of her life first thing in the morning, or she could tell him what she'd come to realise and they could both move on, although God knew where to.

Knowing what she had to do for her own peace of mind as much as Kit's, Lily took a deep breath. 'Not really,' she said and felt the release of a kind of pressure she hadn't realised had been building up inside her.

Kit sat up, alert and to all appearances in something of a state of shock. 'What?'

'There's no need to look quite so surprised,' she said, although she couldn't really blame him given how, at the time, she'd totally laid the responsibility for what he'd done at his door. 'I've had plenty of time over the years to think and I've come to realise that what happened between us wasn't your fault. Or at least not entirely.'

'Really?'

She nodded and broke off a piece of bread. 'Oh, I know what I said then, and I know I laid the blame for it all going wrong wholly at your feet, but that wasn't very fair of me.'

'Wasn't it?' he said, his astonishment fading and leaving the expression on his face totally unreadable.

'You know it wasn't. And you told me so, many times. Not that I was willing to listen. At the time all I could focus on was what you'd done and I didn't think about what might have led to it.' She popped the bread into her mouth, chewed for a moment and then swallowed. 'I mean, you're not the cheating sort, Kit, but I was so blinded by hurt, so wrecked by the feeling of betrayal, I didn't see that. I didn't ask myself why you'd done it and I didn't think about my role in everything. As far as I could see I didn't have a role other than as the only victim. I'd been going through hell and you didn't seem to understand.'

'I tried.'

'I know you did.'

'But maybe not enough.'

'Maybe I didn't let you.'

He rubbed a hand along his jaw. 'With hindsight I should have been firmer and I should have made us face things together.' He let out a humourless laugh. 'But believe it or not I wasn't having all that much fun either.'

'I realise that now.' She sighed. 'But the whole IVF thing was so grim and painful and devastating and by its very definition so physically mainly about me that I failed to see it involved both of us. Plus I knew how much you wanted children being an only child and things, and the knowledge that I couldn't have them just about broke me apart. I didn't cope with things very well and I shut you out.'

'I allowed you to.' Kit shoved his hands through his hair and frowned. 'I told myself that I was giving you space but in reality I think what I was doing was avoiding something I didn't have a clue how to handle.'

It was the first time he'd acknowledged his contribution to the collapse of their marriage and it warmed a part of her deep inside that had always been so cold.

'Really we were both victims, weren't we?' she mused, feeling an odd sense of calm spread through her. 'Of something we didn't have the strength or maturity or understanding to deal with.' She paused. 'Of course you topping things off by going and sleeping with someone else didn't exactly help.'

As her words hung between them Kit paled beneath his tan. 'I'll never forgive myself for that,' he said, his voice cracking a little. 'There's this nugget of guilt that's always there and I'm so sorry, Lily. For everything. But particularly for betraying your trust like that.'

'You're forgiven.'

'Am I?'

'Yes.'

'Are you sure?'

'Of course.' She took a quick sip of champagne. 'Five years is too long to be angry and resentful and I think I forgave you ages ago. I get now that you must have been feeling lonely and isolated and all those other things you said at the time,' she said, remembering the endless evenings she'd spent going over it all. 'That doesn't mean what you did didn't devastate me, because it did. But I can sort of see how it happened. I mean, we hadn't had sex for months, had we? And we were barely speaking. We were virtual strangers. Something had to give at some point.'

His jaw tightened and shadows flickered across his face. 'Nevertheless I made that choice to cheat,' he said gruffly. 'I was the one that trampled all over our marriage vows.'

'True.'

'I've regretted it ever since.'

'Did you ever consider not telling me?'

'For about a nanosecond.'

She tilted her head and looked at him. 'Was it really just sex and a one-off?'

'Yes.'

'Then maybe it would have been better if you hadn't.'

'Perhaps.'

'Although our marriage was dead in the water long before that, wasn't it? So the end result would probably have been the same.'

'If I'd thought there was any hope of salvaging it I'd never have done what I did,' said Kit.

'Wouldn't you?'

'No. Not that it's any excuse. Nothing excuses it. Certainly none of the justifications I came up with.'

Lily winced as everything he had accused her of— self-absorption, surliness, lack of understanding among others—all came back. 'I guess we both said things we probably shouldn't have.'

'Probably,' he said with a nod. 'But I've had time to think too and I was too quick to absolve myself of any of the blame. Whatever was happening to us, I should have made us deal with it together. I regret the fact that I didn't.'

For a moment they lapsed into silence, the space between them no longer filled with regret but a sort of tentative understanding.

'Listen to us,' she said softly, 'each trying to take the blame for the way things turned out.'

'Unlike when it actually happened when all we could do was blame each other.'

'Exactly.'

Kit smiled, his eyes glittering in the candlelight. 'Who'd have thought we'd get so wise?'

'Well, I've had a lot of time to think and I ended up figuring that for me it was like someone—you—had died or something because the man I knew would never have done something like what you did. So I kind of went through the whole grief thing, starting with shock and rage. It took me a while and a *lot* of wine to get round to the acceptance and forgiveness stage but I got there. And here we are, I guess.'

Kit didn't say anything to that, but just looked at her for several long, heavy moments, his eyes darkening and the expression on his face changing into something that made her heart thud and her throat tighten.

'What?' she asked, her voice husky.

'You're incredible.'

'No, I'm not,' she said, trying to tamp down the surge of heat rising up inside her and the thudding of her heart. 'Just a bit older maybe and appreciating the benefit of twenty-twenty hindsight. Anyway, it isn't all one-sided. Didn't you say you'd been thinking too?'

'I've had my moments.'

She shot him a rueful smile. 'And it's not like I didn't do things I regret.' Her smile faded and she bit her lip as a familiar wave of shame rolled through her. 'I'm sorry about cutting up your clothes and keying the Porsche, Kit.'

'Don't be.'

'And the email was truly unforgivable. I should never ever have done that.'

Kit shrugged. 'Water under the bridge.'

Not for her. Once the initial surge of triumphant satisfaction had faded she'd felt sick and hollow and riddled with guilt. Still did a bit. 'Did it make things very difficult?'

'Pretty tough.'

She inwardly cringed. 'What did you do?'

'Having been informed of my questionable integrity none of the British banks would lend me anything and the venture capitalists wouldn't touch me with a bargepole so I went to the States.'

'I read that your first hotel was in New York. I wondered about that. Will you tell me how you did it?'

And so, over the course of dinner, Kit did. He told her how after New York he'd moved to Paris and set up a hotel there. And then, most recently, London.

He told her of the satisfaction he felt of realising the dream he'd had ever since his jet-set parents had taken an apartment in Claridges, the dream that had sustained him through his degree in hotel management and his swift climb up the ladder. He shared the obstacles he'd faced and the successes he'd had.

And in return Lily told him how she'd come to start her business, how shortly after their divorce she'd resigned from her much-loved marketing job. How, needing the distraction of a new challenge, she'd hit upon the idea of offering a range of products to help businesses improve their customer experience. She'd put it to Zoe, who'd been keen, and that was that.

She asked after his parents, and he learned that Zoe was engaged. They discussed a few previously mutual friends with whom only one of them had stayed in touch, the places they'd lived, and caught up on as much as they could while skirting round the subject of lovers in her case and lack of them in his.

Dinner was delicious. At least Lily had told him it was. Personally Kit couldn't taste a thing. He was too busy reeling from everything she'd admitted between their aperitifs and the arrival of the food. Too busy recovering from the mind-blowing discovery that she'd forgiven him and that the second chance he'd so badly wanted might be closer than he'd dared hope. Too busy revelling in the sound of her voice and her laugh, watching her expressive face and losing himself in the depths of her mesmerising eyes. And too busy realising that there was no longer any doubt about whether or not he loved her.

He was absolutely nuts about her. She was the strongest, toughest, most beautiful woman he'd ever met and he was a fool to have ever let her go. He'd never fallen out of love with her and he was going to do everything in his power to win her back.

But he couldn't barge in and tell her what he wanted, he thought suddenly, watching Lily drain the last of her coffee and stifle a yawn. He couldn't carry on with the strategy he'd employed up until now. He was going to have to tread carefully. Their relationship was so fragile, their truce so new, and he could so easily screw things up with his impatience, his need to be in control and his continual drive to move things forwards.

It might be the challenge of the century but with Lily he had to switch mindsets. He had to take a back seat and wait. He had to let her come to him, and then they could begin to build their relationship from there.

So there'd be no more chasing. No more persuading her to do things she didn't really want to do. No more doing anything that might scare her off.

Whatever happened next had to be her decision. All he could do was ensure that he did his best to help her make the one he wanted.

Despite her initial misgivings the evening really couldn't have gone any better, thought Lily, walking beside Kit as he escorted her back to her villa, the inky darkness of the night wrapping round them like a warm, cosy blanket.

Once they'd moved on from the difficult topic of their mess of a marriage, accompanied by course after course of heavenly food and delicious wine, the banter had batted back and forth with barely a break for breath. They'd had so much to talk about, so much to find out. It had been just like old times, but somehow better.

As they'd begun to get to know the people they'd become, Lily had found herself liking Kit more and more, and beneath one lethal smile after another she'd felt herself fall deeper and deeper under his spell.

She'd known it was happening, known that she was being foolhardy and reckless in not bothering to resist, but it had been such a long time since she'd felt like this, all relaxed and languid yet buzzing at the same time, that she hadn't been able to stop herself.

And hadn't really wanted to because over the course of the evening the answers to the questions she'd spent this afternoon trying to figure out had become increasingly clear, and now it seemed that the night held myriad possibilities.

Possibilities that had her body thrumming with anticipation and her heart thumping crazily because dinner had cleared the air. Cleaned the slate. Had maybe, even, reset their relationship, put them back at the start and cleared the way for a stab at a second chance together, free from and prepared for all the trouble that had come their way the first time round.

The idea was kind of thrilling, she thought, going all shivery and hot inside. Exciting. And what she wanted.

What Kit wanted, however, was completely up in the air. He'd been silent and thoughtful ever since he'd offered to walk her back, and infuriatingly wasn't giving anything away.

But if he was as achingly aware of her as she was of him

then there was only one logical conclusion to tonight, and even though on some dim and distant level she knew the idea of falling into bed with him again needed way more consideration, the desire simmering inside her was too insistent to ignore.

'You know, if I'd known how cathartic getting all that stuff off my chest was going to be, I'd have been in touch with you years ago,' said Lily a little huskily as they strolled up the path to her villa.

'Would you?' he murmured.

'Absolutely. I feel as if I've spent the last five years carrying this enormous kind of weight that's suddenly gone. I feel lighter somehow. Calmer.'

'I know what you mean.'

'I'm glad we talked. And had the chance to catch up,' she added with a smile.

'So am I.'

At her door she turned to him and lifted her face, her pulse hammering so hard he must surely be able to see it. Would surely act on it.

'So what happens now?' she said, the anticipation and excitement zipping through her making her all trembly inside.

'Now?' he said, reaching out a hand and softly running his forefinger down her cheek.

She nodded and held her breath as every one of her senses focused on him and this moment.

He tilted his head, his eyes dark and unfathomable. 'Well, sweet pea, that rather depends on you.'

'Me?' she echoed softly, the endearment and his touch stealing her ability to think straight.

He nodded and gave her a faint smile. 'That's right. So have a think about it and let me know.'

And just as she was about to ask what he meant Kit bent his head, dropped a light kiss on her cheek and then, to her utter bewilderment, turned and walked off into the night.

CHAPTER SEVEN

LILY DIDN'T SLEEP WELL—largely because she'd spent most of the night tossing and turning while her body hummed with frustration and unsatisfied desire and her mind churned with confusion—and when dawn broke she was still wide awake, the questions that had plagued her all through the night still rattling around her head.

What on earth was Kit playing at? she wondered, staring up at the slowly rotating ceiling fan that hung over her bed and listening to the soft whirr it made.

Last night she could have sworn he'd been as aware of her as she had of him. She'd been convinced that the practically tangible tension and attraction had been mutual. And what with the endearment, the one she hadn't heard for years, and the touch to her cheek, a gesture so familiar and so missed it made her heart ache just to think about it now, she'd been certain he'd ask to come in for a nightcap, and equally certain that she'd say yes.

But how wrong she'd been. How disappointingly, confusingly wrong.

After the urgency of what had happened in her hall last week and the way he'd crossed half the globe to come and find her—not to mention the interest she'd thought he'd displayed over dinner—the fact that he'd suddenly backed off baffled the hell out of her. She hadn't been expecting—or wanting—the restraint she'd got, the chaste little kiss, nor the tossing of the ball neatly into her court.

And what was that all about anyway?

What had he meant when he'd said that what happened next was up to her? Why was it up to her? And up to her how?

What was he expecting her to do? Make a move? Jump his bones or something? Well, that was never going to happen without some kind of signal from him, she thought darkly. Not now. No way. She needed to know how he felt about her before she made herself vulnerable like that again. She needed to know that there was more to this than just sex.

And unfortunately she didn't, because, while last night she'd had all kinds of ideas about how he might feel about her and had been so ready to drag him into her bed, this morning she didn't have a clue. For all she knew the endearment and the touch had merely slipped out of him from habit and meant nothing.

So where did they go from here? Where did she want them to go? Where did *he?*

Bending her head from side to side to stretch out the kinks in her neck, Lily frowned. Gosh, why was this so difficult? So complicated?

With a sigh of resignation and despair because she was now more at sea than at any point since he'd reappeared in her life, Lily swung her legs round and got off the bed.

Whatever was going on, she thought, heading into the bathroom and flicking on the shower, she had no doubt she'd soon find out, because given the way Kit had gone about things so far it was surely only a matter of time before he turned up demanding to know what she was going to do with that ball.

Or perhaps it wasn't.

Two hours later Lily had had breakfast—by herself— and had hovered by the pool for plenty long enough to be

found, but to her agitation and disappointment there was
no sign of Kit anywhere.

Where was he? Busy? Avoiding her?

Or had he left?

Maybe he had, thought Lily, lowering the e-reader that
she'd been staring unseeingly at for the last ten minutes,
and frowning with distaste as the idea shot into her head
and took root.

Perhaps she'd been too idealistic in her assumption that
they'd cleaned the slate. Perhaps her confession over supper put him off or something. She couldn't really see why
it would, and the ease of their subsequent conversation
hadn't given her that impression, but with hindsight she
had rather let it all out without letting him get much of a
word in edgeways.

Perhaps their conversation, the understanding they'd
reached and the catch-up they'd had was exactly what he'd
been after—closure—and now he'd got it he was done.

Maybe he was after nothing more than friendship or
something and he was perfectly happy for her to let him
know what she thought about that once back in London.

Maybe the kiss he'd dropped on her cheek had been not
one of restraint but one of goodbye.

Her heart squeezed and her throat tightened. Then she
gave herself a quick shake and pulled herself together because on the other hand it was entirely possible she was
being a bit melodramatic about where he could be.

Surely Kit wouldn't have flown all the way out here just
to leave less than twenty-four hours later. Hadn't he said he
was on holiday? And surely he'd want to hang around to
hear what decision she'd come to, even though she hadn't
come to one because she still couldn't figure out what she
was supposed to be deciding.

For her own peace of mind, though, and out of respect
for the author of the book she was struggling to concentrate

on, maybe she'd better go and check if he was still here. Then at least she'd know one way or another and would know how to proceed.

Putting her e-reader down and reaching for her sarong, Lily got to her feet and headed inside.

'Good morning,' she said to the receptionist, with a sunny smile that totally belied the weird kind of tension now clutching at her stomach. 'I was wondering, could you tell me whether Christopher Buchanan has checked out?'

'Not to my knowledge, madam,' he replied.

'Oh, thank God for that,' she said, clapping her hand to her chest and letting out a rush of breath as the tension dissipated and she filled with an overwhelming sense of relief. More overwhelming than the situation warranted, probably, but who cared?

'Would you like to know where he is?'

'I would.' Very much. Because if he wasn't coming in search of her, she'd go in search of him.

'I believe he went to the spa.'

'Thank you.'

Phew, she thought, leaving the main building and walking along the track towards the thatched structure that contained the spa. Kit hadn't gone. He was just having some time out. Relaxing. Doing what millions of people all over the world did on holiday.

Although choosing to do it in a spa did seem kind of incongruous. She'd always thought of him as a man of action and purpose, constantly on the move and unstoppable in his drive for more. He'd never been one for navel-gazing and just sitting around doing nothing, but maybe he'd changed in that respect too. It had been five years after all, and no one— not even Kit—could keep up the kind of level of both mental and physical activity she associated with him for ever.

And even though the idea of him lounging in a steam room or having a massage or something was difficult to reconcile with the Kit she'd once known, she found it surprisingly easy to visualise.

In her mind's eye she could see him sitting on one of the wooden ledges, leaning back against the wall while the steam swirled around him. She could see droplets of water forming on his chest, trickling down over the smattering of hair that covered his skin there, tracing the ripples of his abs and then meandering south before melting into the top of the towel wrapped round his waist.

She could see him closing his eyes and dropping his head back, and her mouth actually began to water as she imagined leaning over and pressing her lips to the skin of his shoulder to catch a droplet and then make the journey it would have made with her tongue.

Right the way down...

At the image of what she might do then, a bolt of heat shot through her, nearly wiping out her knees, and she had to grip the door to the spa for support.

Good Lord.

Feeling faintly dizzy, Lily gave herself a quick shake to dispel the image, determinedly ignored the heat and cleared her throat. She hadn't fantasised like that in years and had no business doing so now. She wasn't seeking Kit out to drool all over him or to melt into a puddle of lust at his feet; she was going after him to see if she couldn't find out a bit more about what he thought was going on here.

Five minutes later she'd found him. Not in the steam room, thank goodness, but in the Jacuzzi. Which actually wasn't all that much better. Because he was naked.

Well, perhaps not entirely naked, she had to concede once her stupefied brain had started working again and the common-sense robbing flush of heat had subsided. Seeing as how the spa was a public space presumably he had

swimming shorts on. Not that she had any intention of in-
vestigating *that* too closely.

Which was just as well as her eyes seemed to have fixed
on his chest and rather worryingly weren't going anywhere,
south or otherwise. The way he was sitting, with his arms
outstretched and resting on the edge of the pool while water
bubbled and popped all round him, displayed it in all its
glory, and she couldn't tear her eyes away.

It was a good chest, she thought dazedly, every nerve
ending she had tingling with awareness. Better now, if that
was possible, than when she'd first become acquainted with
it. His shoulders were broader, his muscles looked harder,
more defined, and his skin was a fraction darker.

Her head filled with the memory of how he'd felt moving
against her, on top of her, inside her and her fingers itched
with the need to reach out and touch him and find out if he
still felt the same, still responded to her in the same way…

It was only when one of her feet actually inched forwards that she jerked back to her senses.

Honestly, what was going on? This was ridiculous. It
was Kit. Her ex-husband. She knew every inch of his body,
from the thick dark hair on his head to his toes and everything in between, so why was she lusting over him as if
she'd never seen a body like it?

Ignoring the knowledge that it was the bits in between
that were causing her such a problem right now, Lily pulled
her shoulders back and dragged her eyes up. To find him
watching her with an annoyingly knowing little smile playing at his lips, the likes of which made her all the more determined to stay cool and in control.

'Hi there,' she said brightly. Overly brightly possibly.

'Good morning.'

'Did you sleep well?' she asked, and immediately wished
she hadn't because all it did was conjure up the memory of

her and Kit falling asleep in each other's arms, hot, satiated and limp with exhaustion.

And then another, of her waking up alone and sad and aware that while physically he was just across the hall in the spare room emotionally they were a million miles apart.

'Like a log,' he said with an easy smile that suggested he wasn't nearly as similarly burdened. 'You?'

'Beautifully,' she lied, ruthlessly dismissing the memories and trying to concentrate. 'I didn't see you at breakfast.'

'I had it in my room.'

'Oh.'

'I had some work to catch up on.'

'Right.'

Then her train of thought faded because, gosh, it was hard work keeping her eyes on his and not letting them drift down as they kept trying to do. And verging on impossible to hold back the urge to whip off her sarong and leap into the Jacuzzi with him and make herself stay where she was.

This was absolutely awful, she thought a little desperately. She'd always been drawn to his body, had always known that the magnetism that existed between them was hard to ignore, but what was going on here was another thing entirely. This was an attraction that she could almost taste. It was intoxicating. Addling. Becoming frighteningly irresistible.

'Did you want something, Lily?'

Him. She wanted him. With a need that was almost blinding. And one that she had to resist until she knew how he felt and what he wanted. For her sanity, her self-respect and her sense of self-preservation. But, goodness, it was going to be hard.

'Lily?'

She blinked and came to. 'What? Oh. Yes.' Although right now she couldn't really remember what it was she wanted. Something to do with finding out what was going on in his head, perhaps.

Well, that was clearly out of the question when her own head was such a mess. She could barely think straight. And if she did embark on the kind of conversation she'd been vaguely contemplating she had the horrible feeling that if he admitted they were done, she might well be reduced to begging, which didn't appeal in the slightest.

She needed time to get used to the situation as well as the scorching attraction she felt for him before attempting a deep and meaningful conversation about what he wanted from her. She needed to see how the land lay a little longer and give him a chance to play his hand first.

So maybe now wasn't the time to go in guns blazing.

'I was thinking,' said Lily, feeling a fraction calmer now she'd come to some kind of a decision about how to handle him and the situation, 'when you're done here, what are your plans for the rest of the day?'

'I don't have any.'

She blinked, faintly taken aback because this was the second time that Kit had surprised her recently. He didn't have plans? That was unusual. It seemed to her that recently he had plans for everything. 'None at all?'

'None at all. Why do you ask?'

'Oh, well, I was thinking of going fishing.' Huh? Was she? That was news to her. Given she'd never done it before she didn't even know if she liked fishing.

'That's nice.'

'And I was wondering if you'd like to join me.'

He shot her a friendly, casual smile that for some reason made her want to slap him. 'Why not?'

Fishing went swimmingly. So swimmingly, in fact, that the following day Lily suggested a tour of the island. Which was such a success that the day after that she and Kit went diving.

The experiences were fabulous, exhilarating, fun, the fishing unexpectedly so. The tour of the island had been fascinating, and when they'd gone diving she'd been overwhelmed by the beautiful and exotic marine life she'd never encountered on any of the dives she'd done before.

What was going on between her and Kit, however, was not so fabulous. Or exhilarating. Or fun. Instead it was downright perplexing.

Three days into their holiday, and Lily didn't know what was going on now any more than she had at the beginning of the week. She and Kit spent all day together, ate every meal together, yet went to bed separately, and, while there had been plenty of laughs and endless conversation, the lie of the land hadn't become any clearer and, more frustratingly, Kit hadn't made any kind of a move.

The word she'd use to describe their relationship at the moment, thought Lily, stuffing a towel into her beach bag and scowling, was platonic.

OK, so most of the activities they'd engaged in hadn't offered the kind of privacy or conditions needed to deal with a potential unstoppable overspill of desire. Such as the day they'd spent fishing and then the tour of the island. On both occasions there'd been other guests and guides around. And when they'd gone diving, yes, there'd been times they'd been alone, but that had generally been underwater, and, while the sight of him in just his swimming shorts had made her stomach flip and her temperature rocket, masks and aqualungs were hardly conducive to either conversation or the intimacy she craved.

But there'd been many an opportunity for non-necessary touching and many a chance of a stolen kiss or two over the last three days. None of which, annoyingly, had been taken up.

They'd never done platonic, and Lily didn't think they should because not being able to touch a body she'd once had permanent and all-over access to, not having the right to it, was driving her nuts.

And that was why over breakfast this morning she'd suggested hiring a speedboat and taking a picnic to one of the private, deserted coves she'd heard of on the other side of the island. That was why she'd dressed in her most flattering bikini, had carefully blow-dried her hair even though it would undoubtedly tangle the minute they set off and had buffed and moisturised every square inch of skin and redone her nail varnish.

She was looking as good as she could under the circumstances, the setting was guaranteed to be conducive to seduction and the food bound to be sublime, and if all of that didn't give him the impetus to make a move, she thought, eyeing herself in the mirror and picking up her bag and hat, then nothing would.

Kit, who was in the resort office and filling in the paperwork relating to the speedboat rental that Lily had suggested earlier, was fast running out of patience. Deciding to wait for her to make up her mind about what she wanted and then let him know was all very well, but at no point had he considered the possibility that she might not. Ever.

But it looked as if that was exactly what was going to happen because he'd been as encouraging as he knew how and yet for three days now she'd shown no interest in him whatsoever. At least none of the sexual kind. And so, while the last few days had been fun and Lily had been great company, he'd slowly been going insane.

He'd seen the look in her eye when she'd happened upon him in the Jacuzzi, and, after thanking the Lord that the lower half of his body was submerged beneath the hot bubbling water and therefore out of sight, had seen it as an encouraging sign.

Fishing, he'd thought, had been an odd choice of activity but he'd been looking forward to it. Looking forward to spending time with her and seeing how she'd handle the attraction that sizzled between them.

But unfortunately she hadn't followed up on the promising start, and day three into his holiday Kit was beginning to wonder why the hell he'd embarked on a strategy of letting her come to him in the first place. And why he wasn't simply abandoning it and dragging her into his arms and to hell with it.

But he couldn't, he reminded himself for what felt like the hundredth time. He had his principles. His strategy was a good one. A necessary one because if they stood any chance of making another go of things it had to be on equal terms. She had to want it as much as he did. Want him as much as he wanted her.

So no way was he going to make the first move. He'd made enough of those already and he was feeling too slavishly in thrall to her as it was. He wasn't going to do a thing until he found out how she felt about him, so if Lily wanted him she could come and get him. The beach they were heading to was quiet. Deserted. Private. They had good food, good wine and the entire day together. All she had to do was give him a sign.

With the paperwork finished, the key in his hand and his resolve once again firm, Kit strode down the jetty to where the boat and picnic were waiting. Climbing aboard and with the morning sun beating down on him, he started carrying out the necessary checks, channelling every drop of his focus into the task and putting his frustrations with Lily from his mind.

Which worked like a dream until he felt his skin prick-

ling with awareness and his muscles tensing and he realised
that she'd arrived.

Forcing himself to relax, he glanced up and flashed her
a quick, cool smile as if the sight of her didn't make his
heart lurch and his mind go blank.

But it did because standing there on the jetty she looked
absolutely incredible. She was wearing some sort of trans-
lucent thing that floated around her body, moulding itself to
her with every breath of breeze and hinting at the luscious
curves beneath. She looked like something out of an ad-
vert. Cool. Gleaming. Gorgeous. And she blew him away.

'Hi,' he said, once he'd managed to regain his power of
speech and gathered the wits she'd scattered.

'Hi.'

Realising that he was in danger of gawking and only a
stone's throw from abandoning his very well-thought-out
and sensible plan, he moved over the deck to where she was
standing and held out his hand.

She took it, and despite his principles, despite his strategy, it was all he could do not to tug her towards him and
'accidentally' have to save her as she overbalanced by wrapping her in his arms.

Once she'd boarded he thought about holding on to her
a fraction longer than was necessary. Saying something
about how beautiful she looked, how sexy he found her.
Giving her hand a squeeze and providing her with the opportunity to squeeze back.

But before he could, she tugged her hand free as if he
were suddenly burning her or something, tore her gaze from
his and then busied herself with stowing her bag beneath
the passenger seat, and he mentally cursed both her for
her indifference and himself for his moment of weakness.

'Ready to go?' he said, feeling his frustration simmer,
his patience thin even more and his mood begin to blacken.

Sitting down and sticking her hat on her head, Lily shot

him a dazzling smile that reminded him he really had to
get a grip of himself if he stood any chance of hanging on
to his self-control today and said, 'I've never been readier
for anything in my life.'

CHAPTER EIGHT

SHE MIGHT BE ready for anything, thought Lily a couple of hours later, but Kit clearly wasn't.

There hadn't been much opportunity for chat when the boat had been speeding through the water, bouncing on the surface, and the wind rushing in her ears, but once they'd dropped anchor and tied up to a buoy, and once they'd waded to the beach, Kit carrying the picnic basket over his head in a particularly manly fashion, she'd thought things would change.

She'd thought that the day would be like the last few days only with an added frisson of tension and anticipation that the privacy of the cove would afford them. She'd thought—perhaps naively—that today would be a good day to initiate a conversation about what they were doing and what they wanted.

But she'd been wrong.

Because judging by the air of surliness that Kit had worn ever since they'd sped away from the jetty and the monosyllabic responses he'd given to her subsequent attempts at small talk he didn't seem up to conversation, let alone the kind of conversation she was toying with.

From time to time, unable to stand the awkward, tense silence, she'd glanced over at him and caught him looking at her with eyes so dark and intense they were utterly unreadable and she'd gone so jittery, breathless and dizzy that she couldn't have spoken even if she'd wanted to.

All in all the morning so far had not been conducive to talking so was it any wonder that every time she'd geed herself up to tackle the conversation she'd planned, she'd chickened out? No, it wasn't.

But perhaps now they'd had lunch he'd be in a better mood, she thought, brightening a little. Maybe he'd just been hungry. Now she thought about it that made a lot of sense because Kit always got grumpy if he was hungry, and it had been quite a while since breakfast. Plus, although he was beginning to stir now, he'd been so still lying beside her, his eyes firmly closed and his breathing slow and deep, she'd guessed he'd had a little sleep, which would surely add to his receptive frame of mind.

So while earlier might not have been the ideal opportunity to talk, maybe now was. Maybe she ought to take the bull by the horns and take advantage of this moment of peace and quiet and seeming calm, and sort things out once and for all.

Lily took a deep breath and summoned her confidence as she rolled onto her side and propped herself up on her elbow. 'Kit?' she said, and smiled at him in what she hoped was a calm, reassuring manner.

Opening his eyes, he turned his head to look at her, ran his gaze the entire length of her and then back up, and abruptly sat up. 'What?' he snapped.

His tone cut through her thoughts, derailing all her plans for talking to him about them and zooming all her attention instead to the look on his face. His features were twisted, as if he were being tortured inside. He looked dark. Wild. Anguished. In agony, in fact.

'Are you all right?' she asked, alarm beginning to shoot through her at the idea that he might be having a seizure or a heart attack or something.

'I'm going for a swim,' he growled, to her astonishment leaping to his feet and striding off towards the sea.

That smile of Lily's would be the ruin of him, thought Kit grimly, slicing through the water in an effort to rid himself of the sizzlingly hot electric energy flowing through him.

All morning she'd been flashing it at him and it had been driving him nuts. Just now, when she'd bestowed it on him again together with that soft murmur and the undulation of her body as she'd rolled onto her side, all gentle hills and tantalising valleys, rises and dips and light and shadow, he'd been within a hair's breadth of reaching for her.

Damn, this whole boat-secluded-beach thing had been such a bad idea. What the hell had he been thinking in agreeing when she'd suggested it? Had he really thought the circumstances would have her throwing herself at him in wild, unbridled passion? Had he really thought he'd have no trouble holding on to his self-control? Hah. What a complete and utterly deluded idiot he'd been. He had no self-control when it came to Lily. He never had.

So what the hell was he going to do now? He couldn't stay out here pounding away at the waves for ever. He had to head back to shore at some point. And what would happen when he did? How was he going to handle this? Did he even want to think about it?

Perhaps it was best not to. Perhaps it was better to just go with his instinct and suffer the consequences. Communicate how he was feeling with actions rather than words. At least then he'd know one way or another how Lily felt, and if she did reject him he could live with it.

With such a strong sense of purpose now calming the heat and tension inside him, Kit turned for the shore. He was halfway there when he stopped for a breath, looked towards the land and saw Lily sitting on the sand in the shallows and clutching her foot, her lovely face contorted in pain.

His blood ran cold and his heart lurched and he started scything through the water just as fast as he could, the desire to find out what was wrong, the need to help her obliterating any kind of other need and desire.

When he reached the shallows he staggered to his feet, his heart pumping and his muscles screaming. Rubbing water from his eyes and pushing his hair back, he stumbled over to her.

'What happened?' he said, dropping to his knees beside her and noting her pale face with concern.

Lily winced and rubbed her foot. 'I was planning to come and join you for that swim but I trod on something sharp.'

'Does it hurt?'

'A bit.' For which he read *a lot*.

'Let me take a look.'

He reached for her foot. He wrapped his hand round her ankle and was about to take her foot in his other when he felt her freeze. He glanced up at her, saw that her eyes were now filling with wariness as well as pain, and he lost what was left of his patience. 'Oh, for heaven's sake, Lily, don't look like that. I'm not going to ravish you.'

'You aren't?'

What did she think he was? Forget communicating with actions rather than words. There wasn't any need for that now. The wariness in her eyes told him everything. She wasn't keen. He got it. Finally. So he'd leave her alone. And not just right here and now. 'Of course not,' he snapped. 'Relax.'

With a nod and a frown she bit her lip and he felt the tension in her muscles ease a little. Dragging his gaze from hers, he gently turned her foot in his hands and tried not to think about the softness of her skin or about how he used to give her foot rubs that frequently turned into something else. He tried not to think about how gorgeous she smelled, how warm she felt or how close her mouth was, so close that all he'd have to do was twist his head, lean forwards and he'd be kissing her.

'Looks like you stood on a sea urchin,' he said, his voice hoarser than he'd have liked.

'Is that bad?'

'I can only see a couple of spines, but who knows?' He racked his brain for what little he knew about the severity of ocean-creature stings and bites but it was hard when his head was filled with nothing but thoughts of what he'd like to do to her. 'Are you having trouble breathing?' He was. In such close proximity to her his lungs seemed to have forgotten how to work.

'No.'

'Chest pain?'

'No.'

'Then probably not.'

He released her foot and got to his feet before he acted on the instinct he'd been favouring only a few minutes ago out there in the sea but was now wholly inappropriate.

'Where are you going?' she asked, squinting up at him.

'There's a bottle of vinegar in the picnic basket. The acid should help.'

She gave him a faint smile. 'Better than you peeing on me, I guess.'

Kit frowned down at her, and thought that despite the stab at humour he didn't like the flush in her cheeks one little bit. 'Don't move.'

'I won't.'

As her foot continued to throb and tiny stabs of pain shot along it Lily watched Kit head over to the picnic basket, her heart contracting and her spirits plummeting.

Her intention to follow him into the sea and continue the conversation she'd barely started might not have worked out as planned, but she'd wanted an answer to the question about where they were heading and now she had it.

Kit wasn't planning to ravish her, and she didn't think he meant simply here on this beach. A minute ago they'd been practically naked and so, *so* close to each other and all he'd shown her was cool practical concern, while she...

She blew out a breath as she watched him hunker down and rummage around in the basket for the vinegar, part of which had dressed the salad and part of which was apparently to dress her, and swallowed back a surge of desire.

Well, she'd lied when she'd told him she wasn't having trouble breathing and didn't have chest pain, although neither had anything to do with standing on a sea urchin.

The minute he'd laid his hands on her and turned her foot with a gentleness she'd never have expected from him her breathing had gone haywire. And then when he'd told her he had no intention of ravishing her her chest had tightened so much her heart had physically hurt.

And now he was coming back with the damn vinegar and she was going to have to employ every drop of self-control she possessed to stop herself throwing caution to the wind and herself into his arms.

Swallowing hard, Lily kept her hands planted on the sand as Kit once again knelt beside her.

'I'll see if I can remove as many of the spines as I can,' he said with a brief smile. 'I'll try to be gentle.'

She didn't want gentle, she thought rebelliously, clamping her lips together to stop the words tumbling out as he held her foot and began pulling out the spines. She wanted rough. Urgent. Desperate. She wanted his hands not touching her in the cool, impersonal manner of a doctor, but stroking her and kneading her and caressing her in the manner of a lover. She wanted hands that would explore her and make her tremble and drive her mindless with desire.

She might have let out a tiny moan. She might have whimpered. Whatever noise she did make Kit instantly stilled, his head jerking up and his gaze locking with hers.

Something flickered in the depths of his dark eyes and her breath caught. For a moment it felt as if the entire world had stopped to see what was going to happen next.

And then he was jerking away from her, snapping the connection of their gazes and shoving a hand through his hair, and the world carried on its business.

'Kit?' she murmured, reeling from the intensity of the moment and the abrupt way it had ended.

'You winced,' he muttered, jamming the lid on the vinegar and standing up. 'I'm sorry if I hurt you. But now you're done.'

'Nothing to worry about,' she said, scrambling to her feet, the pain now wiped out by a wave of mortification and the sting of rejection. 'And thank you.'

'We'd better head back.'

'Good plan.'

Returning from a visit to the clinic, where her foot was checked and given a cleanish bill of health, Lily stalked into her villa, threw her bag on the sofa and then flung herself on the bed, frustration, disappointment and tension practically tearing her apart.

Kit didn't want her. Physically or otherwise. That much was now blindingly obvious. So obvious, in fact, that she was kind of stunned she'd ever got into her head that he did.

How could she have been so stupid, so deluded? Well, her sister had a lot to answer for, she thought darkly, rolling onto her front and burying her head in a pillow. If it hadn't been for that stupid phone call she'd never have leapt to the clearly wrong conclusion that he might still have feelings for her.

Zoe had said she thought that Kit might still love her, but *might* also meant *might not,* didn't it?

And if *that* was the case then she'd been wrong to read so much into the look he'd given her in the bar when she'd first turned up for supper the day he'd arrived. She'd thought she'd seen so much there in his eyes, but perhaps she'd only seen it because she'd wanted to see it. And perhaps she'd been wrong to imagine, wonder, hope even, that things between her and Kit could be anything other than what they were.

Which was absolutely devastating, because while the last few days hadn't resulted in a tumble in the waves, they *had* highlighted all the reasons why she'd fallen in love with him in the first place: his enthusiasm for everything he did; his live-life-to-the-full attitude; the way he made her feel protected and cherished; his generosity and inherent kindness.

They'd also highlighted the fact that despite all her assertions to the contrary, despite everything she'd told herself over the last five long, horrible years, she'd never fallen out of love with him. She knew now that she still loved everything about him. Always had, always would.

While he was completely indifferent to her.

As her heart twisted Lily let out a muffled wail and thumped the mattress with her fists. Oh, what a mess. So much for wondering where they were going, she thought desolately. They weren't going anywhere. Apart from home. Tomorrow. And then on with their lives. Separately.

As a stab of despair shot through her at the futility of it all she rolled onto her back, sat up and looked gloomily out of the window.

At least the weather, having taken a turn for the worse, was vaguely sympathetic to the blackness of her mood.

Ever since they'd got back—and what a hideously awkward journey that had been—the air pressure had been dropping and the temperature had been rising to what was now an almost unbearable level. The clouds that had started scudding across the sky when they'd moored the boat back at the jetty were now so dense and dark it felt as if the island were lying beneath a heavy, hot and humid blanket.

Even though it was only mid-afternoon it felt like dusk. Not the soft, balmy dusk of the last few days, but an edgy, malevolent dusk that was laden with an ominous kind of portent. The wind was whipping up the sea, bending the trees practically double, and the air was crackling with electricity that she could feel vibrating through her too.

She felt weirdly on edge. Prickly. As if a whole hive of bees had taken up residence inside her.

And what exactly was she going to do for the rest of the afternoon? She couldn't read. Couldn't work. Couldn't do any of the activities the resort usually had to offer as everything had been cancelled due to the storm that was brewing. There was the gym, but even if that had appealed Kit had muttered something about heading that way when they got back, which ruled it totally out.

And as for simply lying back and relaxing, well, that was out of the question too because in the absence of anything else to do it seemed that she was going to be spending the afternoon driving herself mad with if onlys and what ifs, wondering what he was thinking, what he was doing and if there was anything she could have done differently to make him want her again. The rest of the time she had left on the island she'd have to spend avoiding him.

Or would she?

A clap of thunder boomed across the sky, rattling the windows and making her jump. And get a grip.

Hang on, she thought, jumping off the bed and beginning to pace as her brain suddenly started whirring. What was she? Some kind of a wimp? Who was this woman who shied away from a challenge? Where was the woman who'd been so determined to have it out with him that she'd accidentally stood on a sea urchin?

Was she really going to meekly accept that they weren't going anywhere and just leave things in the past? Was she really going to give up without knowing for sure that there was no future for them when the opportunity to find out was there for the taking?

No, dammit, she wasn't.

What the hell did she have to lose by confronting him? Her pride? Well, that had gone years ago. Her sense of self-preservation? Hah. She'd been kidding herself that she ever had one in the first place.

And what was she so frightened of? That he might turn her down? Or that he might not?

Lightning split the sky, illuminating the room for a second, and Lily felt her heart begin to race as what she had to do, what she *wanted* to do, became clear.

She couldn't go home not knowing what could have been and she couldn't stand another minute of the uncertainty. And yes, the outcome of what she was about to do was a fairly scary unknown, and yes, the weather was diabolical, but in all honesty, she thought grimly as she grabbed her cagoule and pulled it on, she'd faced far worse.

Making it back from the gym to his villa a second before the heavens opened, Kit strode into the shower room and flicked on the water with perhaps more force than was strictly necessary, but frankly he was all out of patience, and all out of hope.

He'd done his best to get Lily to want him the way he wanted her, but his best simply wasn't good enough. He had to accept the fact that Lily just wasn't interested in him the way he was in her.

The memory of her sitting on the edge of the beach shot

into his head. The moment he'd caught the tiny sound she'd made that could have been pain or something else and their gazes had locked. The highly charged moment in which it had seemed to him that they were teetering on a knife-edge. In which he'd been willing her to take the chance on them. And in which she hadn't.

The moment that had pretty much told him everything he needed to know.

Steeling himself against the stab of pain that struck his chest, he stripped off his gym kit, tossed it into the laundry basket that sat in the corner of the bathroom and stepped into the cubicle.

Switching the water to ice-cold, Kit winced and felt his muscles relax after his workout, but as for the ache in his chest, well, that, he suspected, was going to be more difficult to assuage.

But he'd just have to because he could take a hint. Or lack of. He wouldn't seek Lily out any more. He wouldn't try to change the way things were. It had been a mistake to think that there was any chance of a reconciliation. They had too much baggage and the past should remain right there, in the past.

It had definitely been a mistake to come here, he thought grimly, turning the tap to hot, grabbing the bottle of gel and beginning to lather himself up. With hindsight he'd have stayed the hell away.

But never mind. He only had another twenty-four hours or so on this godforsaken island and then he'd be home. Back to normal. More or less. He'd put Lily out of his mind and get on with his life. He'd move on. Just as he should have once he'd discovered his little 'problem' had been solved. He'd get over the distaste at the thought of meeting someone else. Of course he would. In time.

He'd have to because whatever the future held, one thing was certain: it didn't hold Lily.

What with thunder crashing through the sky, the hammering of the rain on the roof and at the windows and the pelting of the shower over his body—not to mention the rushing in his ears at the acknowledgement that he and Lily really were over—at first Kit didn't hear the pounding on the door of his villa.

Then he did and he frowned because who the hell was out in this weather? And what was so urgent that it couldn't wait until it passed?

With a scowl, he switched off the shower, grabbed a towel and wrapped it round his waist. Feeling so tightly wound he thought he might be about to snap, he stalked out of the bathroom. Headed into the hall.

And stopped dead because—it was Lily.

The last person he wanted to see. The only person he wanted to see.

With an eerie sense of fatalism, Kit walked over to the door, his heart thundering and his stomach churning. He opened it and flinched at the gust of wind that whipped in.

Wearing some kind of waterproof top that didn't have any chance of standing up to the full force of a tropical storm, Lily was sopping wet and dripping onto the step. Her hair was plastered to her skull and her eyes were wild in the dim light of the afternoon. There was a tension gripping her body that drew him. Confused him. Made him wish he were wearing considerably more than just a towel.

Ignoring the disturbing effect she was having on him, he pulled her inside and then with some effort closed the door.

'What the hell are you doing out in this weather?' he growled, deliberately channelling his feelings of frustration and confusion into anger to stop himself from dragging her against him and in all likelihood getting a slap to the face. 'Are you insane?'

'Very probably,' she said with a shiver as she peeled her cagoule off.

He stepped forwards to take it from her and then, before the scent of her could get to him, wheeled off to hang it in the bathroom. He brought back a towel and handed it to her.

She rubbed her hair and all Kit could do was watch and wish he were doing it for her. With his brain a mess and his body a mass of tension and need he didn't trust himself to speak so instead he waited until she was done.

'I knocked for ages,' she said eventually, dropping the towel on the sofa and raking her fingers through her hair.

'I was taking a shower. I didn't hear you.'

'I apologise for the interruption.'

Kit frowned at the shakiness of her voice. It might be hot and humid outside but now he thought about it she sounded cold. Sort of numb.

And then it struck him like the lightning that was now flashing all around them that Lily had always been terrified of storms. At the first crack of thunder she'd always dived beneath the duvet, shivering and sweating and breathing far too fast. The only thing that had calmed her was taking her into his arms and letting her burrow right up against him until it was over.

'Are you all right?' he asked, the desire and frustration hammering through him making way for a thread of concern.

She blinked up at him. 'Of course I'm all right. Why wouldn't I be?'

'You hate storms.'

She stared at him. 'What?'

'You're terrified of them.'

'No, I'm not.'

'You used to be.'

'Oh. Well. Yes. But I saw someone,' she said, linking her hands and, he thought, for some reason holding on tightly. 'Did a course. Got over it.'

'You did a course?'

'Yes.'

'I didn't know that.'

'There are a lot of things that you don't know about me.'

'Clearly.' Such as… 'What are you doing here, Lily?'

For a moment she just looked him. Swallowed. Then pulled her shoulders back. 'OK, well, the thing is…' She paused then took a deep breath. 'The thing is, I want to know what's going on here, Kit.'

At her words Kit went very still and his brain went on high alert. 'What do you mean?'

'With us.'

Wasn't it obvious? He'd thought it was. But maybe it wasn't. His heart began to thump, though with what he didn't know. 'What do you think is going on?'

Lily blew out a breath and threw her hands in the air, as if some sort of dam had burst and she couldn't hold back any more. 'I don't have a clue, do I? First you're all "let me in we need to talk it's urgent" and pushing me up against a wall, next you're rushing halfway across the globe to come and find me, and now you couldn't be less interested. I don't understand it.'

Kit blinked as if he'd just been thumped in the chest. She thought he wasn't interested? Why would she think that when he'd gone overboard trying to show her just how interested in her he was? 'I'm interested,' he said roughly.

She rolled her eyes and crossed her arms beneath her breasts. 'Oh, yes, sure. In a brotherly kind of way.'

His jaw tightened and his eyes narrowed. What the hell? 'You think I'm being brotherly?'

'What else would you call it?' she said, jutting her chin up. 'The constant helping hand and all the buddy-buddy stuff. The sea-urchin-spine-vinegar thing. Not to mention this current seriously misplaced concern for my well-being.'

'Not brotherly,' he said tightly. 'Not brotherly in the slightest.'

'Then what is it?' she said, her cheeks pink and her chest heaving. 'Because it's driving me nuts. Completely nuts. I don't want your help, Kit, and I don't need your concern.'

Kit could feel the rush of blood to his head, the pounding of his heart. 'What do you need, Lily? What do you want?'

'What do you think?'

'Tell me.'

'OK, fine, I miss you.'

He went very still, every cell of his body hovering, waiting. 'We've spent the best part of the last four days together.'

'I miss your touch. I miss your nearness. I miss your kisses.'

'So what's the problem? Sexual frustration?'

'Damn right that's the problem,' she said, her eyes flashing and her breathing going all choppy. 'Partly. You owe me an orgasm.'

'Well, why didn't you say?'

'I'm saying it now.'

He took a step towards her, his eyes not leaving hers. 'Say it all,' he said.

'Everything?'

'Didn't you say that honesty was the best way to deal with this?'

She gulped. Her breath caught. 'These last few days have been hell, Kit.'

'In what way?'

'I want you so badly it's practically eating me up, while you…' She shrugged. 'You just don't seem to feel the same way.'

'I do.'

Her gaze snapped to his. 'You do?'

'Very much so.'

'So what has this all been about?'

'Me needing you to want it as much as I do.'

'I do,' she said, her voice breaking. 'I really do.'

There came a crash of thunder. 'Then show me.'

CHAPTER NINE

LILY DIDN'T NEED telling twice. After all the stress, the uncertainty and the tension that had been churning around inside her, the knowledge that Kit wanted her as much as she wanted him just about undid her, and with her heart pounding madly and heat flooding through her she flew into his embrace.

She threw her arms around his neck and plastered herself against him and held on for dear life as Kit whipped his arms round her waist and crashed his mouth down on hers.

His tongue delved into her mouth, sweeping over hers, tangling with hers, so fiercely, so desperately, that her knees nearly buckled.

As desire rocketed through her she pressed herself close and Kit pulled her even tighter, and she could feel the length of him beginning to harden against her abdomen.

He swept his hand up and buried it in her hair in a move that was so familiar it made her heart ache. Taking matters into her own hands and summoning up the courage to face him had been the best thing she could have done, and battling through torrential rain and gale-force winds, getting soaked, had been worth it. So worth it.

Because she'd missed this so much. Missed him so much. Pressing herself closer, Lily ran her hands down over his shoulders and then his back, tracing the contours of his muscles, feeling him tremble beneath her touch.

Then she reached the towel tied at his waist, and, filling with a longing she could barely contain, she tugged at it until it fell to the floor and he was naked. She dug her fingers into the muscles of his buttocks, pulling him closer and tilting her hips so she could rub herself against him.

Breaking off the kiss and breathing heavily, Kit stared down at her, his eyes hot and dark and glazed with desire, before dropping his hands to the hem of her top and pushing it up. She raised her arms to help him lift it off her and toss it to the floor. And then he was unzipping her skirt and tugging it down together with her knickers and she was stepping out of both and kicking off the trainers she'd donned to make the wet, sandy journey over here.

Pulling her back into his arms, and capturing her mouth with his once again, Kit manoeuvred her round until the backs of her knees hit the edge of the bed and down she went. She fell back onto the soft mattress and he came down on top of her, taking her wrists and pinning her arms to the bed as he kissed her.

She moaned and wriggled but he didn't release her. Instead he tore his mouth from hers and as she panted and gasped for breath he began trailing kisses down her neck and over the slope of her left breast until his mouth closed over her nipple and she couldn't help but abandon all attempts to free herself.

Beneath the force of the electricity and sheer wanton need that was shooting through her, her brain virtually melted and she stopped struggling and simply gave into revelling in the heaven he was taking her to.

Kit moved down her body, his mouth scorching her skin wherever it travelled, until he reached the hot, wet centre of her and she gasped at the heat of his breath over her.

He let go of her wrists, which should have given her the opportunity to touch him the way she'd been so desperate to, but then he was holding her hips still and slowly lowering his head to her and she was going so dizzy with desire that all she could do was clutch at the sheet.

'Hey,' she said softly, hoarsely, trying to make light of what potentially was so overwhelmingly powerful that she feared there might be no going back. 'I thought *I* was supposed to be showing *you* how much I wanted this.'

Instantly stilling, Kit lifted his head, looked up at her and murmured, 'You were. On the other hand, as you so perceptively pointed out, I owe you an orgasm.'

'There is that,' she said dazedly, her mouth dry and her blood roaring in her ears.

'But it's your call.'

As if she were going to stop him now. As if she could move anyway. As if she even wanted to. 'I think I'd better just shut up.'

'Good decision.'

And, boy, it was. As Kit returned his attention to the hot, wet centre of her her eyes fluttered closed and her body vibrated with the sensations rocketing through her.

When his tongue touched her clitoris she arched off the bed with a soft groan. He sucked. Licked. Slid one finger, then another, into her and gently, achingly slowly moved them inside her. Expertly building the tension inside her, knowing exactly how to, speeding up and slowing down until she thought she'd go mad with either desire or frustration.

She moaned. Cried out in desperation. Began to pant and writhe and was practically on the point of begging when Kit combined the licking and the sucking with a clever twist of his fingers and the tight ball of tension deep inside her exploded. And then she was spiralling out of control, hurtling into oblivion and splintering into a billion tiny pieces as she convulsed and clenched around his fingers with his name on her lips.

'That certainly evened up the score,' she mumbled, once

the tremors had subsided, her vision had cleared and she'd got her breath back.

He pushed himself up and took his weight on his elbows as he looked down at her. 'Good.'

'I want more.'

'Demanding.'

She shot him a wicked smile. 'Oh, you have no idea.'

'I'm intrigued.'

'I still need to show you how much I want this. And you.'

'Then what are you waiting for?'

'Absolutely nothing,' she said, curling a leg around his hip and rolling him onto his back.

Straddling his hips, she leaned forwards to kiss him and, taking him in one hand, positioned him and, unable to wait any longer, sank down.

He groaned into her mouth and she gasped at the feel of him stretching her, filling her, so tight, so deep. He began to move but she stilled him.

'Wait,' she said.

'What?'

'Patience, my darling.'

'Not one of my virtues. Although I must say I've astounded myself this last week.'

'Really?'

'Like you wouldn't believe. Not as much as you're astounding me now though.'

'You like this?' she said teasingly.

'I always did. You know that.'

'Me too.'

He reared up then and, clamping one hand to the back of her neck, the other to her hip, held her close. She could feel his heart thudding against her. Inside her. And then unable to help herself she began to move. Rocking slowly against him, rolling her hips forwards as he thrust up.

The rain continued to pound the roof and the terrace, and sweat coated her skin as the heat inside her grew.

Kit brought her head forwards, caught her mouth with his, and she clutched at his shoulders, barely able to stand the pleasure coursing through her. She whimpered. He moaned and she felt the tension, the desperation clawing at her.

'God, Lily,' he said, breaking the kiss for a moment, his breathing harsh and fast and his face tight.

'I know.' She was trembling so much, feeling so much she thought she might burst with the pressure of it.

'I love you,' he said quietly, looking deep into her eyes.

'I love you too.'

And then his grip on her tightened and he was moving harder and faster and she was grinding down onto him and then with one last powerful thrust he buried himself deep inside her. She felt him pulsate and throb, and the vibrations and the words he groaned into her ear tipped her over the edge, her body erupting in ecstasy.

Lying on the sun lounger and gazing up at the canopy of stars with Lily snuggled between his legs, her head resting on his shoulder, both of them wrapped in his sheets, Kit thought it was kind of hard to believe that only a couple of hours ago he'd been considering jacking it all in with her.

At one point he'd been about as low as he could be but now, after the craziest, best afternoon he'd had in years, there were possibilities. Infinite possibilities.

Just as the storm had cleared the heavy tropical air of dust and heat, leaving everything clean and fresh, they'd cleared the air of the doubt and frustration that had lain between them.

Now he and Lily had the chance to make a new start, and he intended to take full advantage of the fact that those doors were no longer merely ajar but wide open.

'Have you really been thinking about this for the last four days?' Lily murmured, cutting into his thoughts as she gently ran her fingers along his forearm, which lay across her beneath her breasts.

'Pretty much every second.'

'I never guessed.'

'Nor I about you.'

'What a lot of time we've wasted.'

Her words held a note of regret and he smiled faintly. 'I don't think so.'

She tilted her head back and round to glance up at him. 'No?'

'Well, put it this way, if we'd done this days ago we'd never have seen or done half the things we have. In all likelihood we wouldn't have left the villa.'

'That's true.'

'I'd never have learnt how good you are at fishing.'

'That was just beginner's luck.'

'We wouldn't have seen the Madagascar anemonefish.'

'We wouldn't. And it was incredible. Still, I'm pretty sure I'd rather have been doing this.'

She had a point. 'Good to see our ability to communicate is as strong as ever,' he said.

'Yeah.'

'When did we get so bad at reading each other?' he murmured, idly stroking his fingers through her hair and feeling her shiver.

'You have to ask?'

He grimaced in the dark. 'Not really.'

More of a gradual descent than a sudden drop, it had started at around the time of the third failed cycle of IVF, he knew. They'd had such hopes. Dashed once again. Unable to deal with the devastating disappointment, Lily had withdrawn into herself, slowly turning into someone he didn't recognise, and as he hadn't had a clue how to help her he'd spent more and more time at work, telling himself he needed to do it in order to move on and up, but, more likely, subconsciously wanting to avoid her, the situation and the disintegration of their relationship.

'Anyway,' she said, pulling him back, 'I think the last couple of hours proved that we've rediscovered the art.'

They had indeed. Their bodies instinctively recognised each other. Moved together as if they'd never been apart. He remembered what she liked with barely any effort of thought and she remembered what drove him wild.

A gentle gust of wind ruffled her hair and he felt it slide against his fingers like silk. 'I like this,' he said.

'My hair?'

'It suits you short.'

'Thank you.'

'When did you change it?'

'Years ago.'

'A new start?'

'Something like that.'

'Why did you never remarry, Lily?'

At his question, Lily went still, tensed a little, then relaxed in the kind of way that felt as if it had taken some effort. 'Oh, I don't know,' she said lightly. Too lightly, he thought. 'Once bitten, twice shy, maybe.'

'That's all?'

Where the question had come from Kit had no idea, but now it was out there he was rather interested, rather hoping she'd admit that she'd never truly got over him.

She sighed. 'No. Not really.'

'Then why?'

'I never met anyone.'

'Seriously?' He found that rather hard to believe. Lily was gorgeous. Fun. Successful. He'd have thought she'd have been snapped up within weeks. Was very glad she hadn't.

'To be more accurate I suppose I never let myself meet anyone,' she said, twining her fingers through his. 'At least not anyone I could be properly interested in.'

Kit frowned, unable to work that out. 'What do you mean?'

'I guess I always figured a deep and meaningful relationship would put me in a vulnerable position or something. I didn't—don't—ever want to be in a situation again which could lead to the kind of pain and heartache and desolation I went through with you. Does that make any sense whatsoever?'

'More than it should. So what are you saying? You've been celibate all these years?'

'No, of course not,' she said with a soft laugh that clearly didn't take into consideration the jealousy lancing through him at the thought of her with other men. 'I've been out with guys. Nice guys. Had flings and things. But none of them involved the earth-moving, mind-shattering, fireworks-and-explosions kind of sex we had. It was more a case of the scratching of an itch. Which suited me just fine at the time.'

'But not now?'

She turned her head and smiled up at him. 'What do you think?'

Kit thought that she was never having sex—good or bad—with anyone else ever again.

'Anyway, what about you?' she said. 'Why haven't you ever remarried? You always did want children and it can't have been for lack of opportunity.'

'It wasn't.'

'Silly me for asking.'

The trace of jealousy in her voice made him smile. 'But every relationship I've attempted tended to be hampered by the problem you solved on New Year's Eve.'

'Your impotence?'

He winced. 'Ouch. Do you have to?'

'Sorry,' she said, not sounding sorry at all. 'What would you call it?'

'A temporary psychological problem to do with certain issues relating to intimacy.'

'Not all that temporary if it went on for five years.'

'No.'

'And that sounds like something a therapist would say.'

'It was.'

Shifting out of his embrace, she sat up and turned round to stare at him, surprise written all over her face. 'You saw a therapist?'

'I did.'

'But it didn't help?'

'Nothing did.'

'That must have been frustrating.'

'You have no idea.'

'Well, now you're cured you can go back and take your pick.'

Kit looked at her thoughtfully. 'I could,' he said eventually. 'But I won't.'

She went very still, not taking her eyes off him for a second. 'Oh?'

'Because this—us—isn't just sex, is it?'

'I don't think so,' she said, so softly it came out as almost a whisper. 'I've spent the entire last week remembering why I fell in love with you.'

'Ditto.'

'And now I think the real reason that I've never really had a proper relationship since us is that despite everything I tried to tell myself I never fell out of love with you.'

'And I think that the problem I had with sex, which I always thought was to do with the guilt I carried at having that one-night stand, was down to the fact that I never fell out of love with you.'

She tilted her head, a faint smile playing at her lips. 'What a pair we are.'

They could be a formidable pair, thought Kit. A great pair. And if only she gave him the chance to prove it, he'd devote the rest of his life to making up for what he'd done to her and to them. He took a deep breath, his heart hammering so wildly he could feel it banging against his ribs. 'Lily?'

'Yes?'

'What would you say to us trying again?'

Despite the fact that somewhere in the back of her mind Lily had been expecting something like this, she still had to bite back the 'yes' that was trying to tumble out of her mouth, and she still had to clamp down on the urge to throw herself against him and smother him in kisses.

Because while she'd thought about it quite a lot this afternoon, and fantasised about it before that more than she cared to admit, the reality of them wasn't some kind of fairy tale. It wasn't all hearts and roses, lost love found and a blissful happy ever after.

Once upon a time it had been painful, heartbreaking and soul-destroying. Now it was messy and filled with memories and experiences that were not, perhaps, conducive to a healthy, functional relationship.

So while on one level the idea that they got back together was the best thing she'd heard in ages, on another she had so many doubts and fears about what would happen if they did that she held back.

Ignoring her heart, which was remembering he'd said he loved her, Lily listened to her head, which was insisting she proceed with caution, and sighed. 'I don't know, Kit.'

He frowned, his smile fading. 'What don't you know? You know I love you.'

'And I love you. But we were in love last time and look

what happened. What makes you think it would work this time round?'

'We've changed.'

'Enough?'

'I think so.'

He was right. They had. But still… 'Some things haven't though.'

'Like what?'

'Like the children you've always wanted,' she said, and steeled herself for the dull ache that throbbed through her. Not quite the sharp pain it had been because she'd come to terms with it now, but nevertheless it still hurt a little. 'That's not going to happen with me, because I really don't think I could go through the whole IVF thing again.'

Three rounds had been quite enough and she never again wanted to experience the hope and the despair that the procedures had aroused in her. Never again wanted to be reminded of the pain and devastation of her ectopic pregnancy and her resultant infertility.

'There are other options,' he said, watching her closely.

'Adoption?'

He'd suggested that once before, just after she'd found out that the third round of treatment hadn't worked, and at the time she'd been feeling so like she'd failed in her evolutionary role on the planet, and so unable to believe that he could have brought it up at that time, that she'd yelled at him that he was unthinking and unfeeling and wholly insensitive if he thought that adopting could make up for holding their own child in her arms.

But now, though, she could see that it was an option. The only one they had really.

'We could think about it,' he said. 'At some point. Or not. Whatever you want. I'd rather have you and no children than a family with anyone else. I always did.'

Ignoring the warmth that swept through her at that, Lily

said quietly, 'You say that now, but what if you change your mind?'

'I won't.'

'You might.'

'Trust me.'

'And that's another thing,' she said, frowning as yet another thing to worry about should she agree to try things again flew into her head. 'How do I know I *can* trust you? How do I know that when things get tough, when I go all weird and withdrawn, as I'm bound to from time to time, you won't go and find comfort with someone else?'

He reached out and took her into his arms. Pulled her round and back into him, nestling her head beneath his chin. 'Because we'll talk,' he said against her hair as he held her tight. 'Communicate.'

'Do you think we can?'

'I'll make sure we do. I won't let us not.'

Lily watched a shooting star dart across the sky and felt her heart skip a tiny beat. 'Is it really that simple?'

'It could be if we take things one day at a time.'

At the sincerity in his voice and with the warmth and heat of his body wrapped round her Lily found herself hovering.

Could they make a go of it? Get it right this time? Kit did make it sound simple. And out here, in the velvety isolation of the night, tucked away in their own little bubble, it seemed as if anything was possible.

But what would it be like when they got back to London? Back to life? Real life. Would they be able to navigate the obstacles of their relationship as well as two busy careers? Not to mention manage the expectations of family and friends. Did they have the strength? The commitment? Did they really have the ability to be open and honest when experience suggested otherwise?

'Look, Lily, I'm not saying it won't be hard,' he said

quietly, as if able to read her mind. 'I don't think we're always going to have an easy ride. All I know is that I love you and if I do by some miracle get you back I'll do my damnedest to make it work.'

At the quiet conviction of his words and with the beat of his heart strong and steady beneath her shoulder she could feel herself falling. 'I'd need honesty.'

'You'd have it.'

'Always?'

'Always. And I won't give you any reason not to be able to trust me. Ever.'

'Really?'

'I promise.'

And just like that down she went, head over heels into a future with him. 'All right,' she whispered with her heart in her throat. 'Let's do it.'

CHAPTER TEN

'You look happy.'

Lily dropped her bag on her desk, sat down in her chair and gave her sister a smile that was wide and bright and at the moment pretty much permanent. 'I am.'

And she was. Because despite her misgivings, the last couple of months had been wonderful. Better than she could ever have imagined. And so much fun that every time she thought about the five years she and Kit had been apart she found herself shaking her head in amazement that she'd actually thought she'd been fine.

She hadn't been fine, she could see now. She'd been coasting. Simply existing as the days rolled endlessly by, and living her life in black-and-white. And despite a great social life and her fabulous family, she'd been so very, very lonely.

In contrast, since they'd returned from the Indian Ocean she felt as if she were on fire. She woke up every morning raring to go, brimming with a fizzing sort of energy she could barely contain. The days now whizzed by in glorious Technicolor, the nights were hot and heavy with passion and she'd never felt less lonely or more convinced that choosing to give them a second shot had been the best decision she'd ever made.

Not that everyone thought so. Her parents, for example, had been extremely wary, not wanting to burst her bubble of happiness yet unable to refrain from suggesting proceeding with caution. But that was only natural given that they'd seen the wreck she'd been when she and Kit had parted.

And while most of her friends had been carefully congratulatory, others, who'd also witnessed her falling apart, told her she was mad and wanted to know how she was able to trust him, to which she would shrug and say she just did.

The only person who seemed genuinely delighted was Zoe, who was so loved-up at the moment and so wrapped up in wedding plans that she was delighted by pretty much everything these days.

'Happier than usual, now I come to think of it,' said Zoe, dragging Lily out of her musings and back to the office where she was supposed to be picking up information for her imminent meeting.

'That's entirely possible,' said Lily, reaching for the folder she needed that was lying on her desk and putting it in her bag-cum-briefcase.

'What's happened?'

She zipped her bag. 'Kit asked me to move in with him.'

'And?'

'I agreed.'

Zoe blew out a breath. 'Wow.'

'I know. Great, isn't it? Although I suggested he move in with me. I mean, he lives in a hotel. I rattle round a four-bedroomed house.'

'And he was all right with that?'

Lily nodded and swivelled to her computer to quickly check where she was going. 'Seems to be,' she said, pulling up the maps page and entering the postcode. 'I mean, he has most of his stuff there already and it's not like we haven't done it before. I already know his bad habits and of course I don't have any.'

Zoe grinned. 'Of course you don't. So when does he move in?'

'Next weekend.' And she couldn't wait.

'Things are going well, then?'

'Yup.'

'I'm glad. You know, I always liked him.'

'Did you?' asked Lily, glancing up at her sister and shooting her a quick smile. 'Because I seem to remember you once saying that hanging, drawing and quartering was too good for him.'

Zoe waved a dismissive hand. 'That was years ago in response to a very specific circumstance. Things are different now.'

'They are,' she agreed, thinking that they were different indeed.

For one thing they'd already been through more stuff than most people had to deal with in a lifetime of marriage, and had come through. For another *they* were different. This time round they were their own people. They weren't wrapped up in each other to the exclusion of everyone else, as she'd realised they had been before. They were more mature, more settled, more grounded. Their relationship was now more adult. In more ways than one, she thought, drifting off for a very happy moment to remember some of the new tricks she and Kit had tried in the bedroom, the bathroom, the kitchen…

'Dan likes him too,' said Zoe, snapping Lily out of her delightful little reverie.

'The feeling's entirely mutual.'

Her ex-husband and her future brother-in-law had got on like a house on fire when they'd first met. Now they played squash together on a pretty regular basis, which was faintly weird, although great.

'So what have you got lined up for today?'

Lily sat back, her smile deepening. 'We're going on a date. Kit's off to Rome tomorrow to check out a site for a new hotel so he's taking me to this brand-new restaurant that's opened just around the corner from home. It's very cool and very difficult to get a table.' But he'd done it. For her.

Zoe grinned and rolled her eyes. 'I meant *today* today. As in workwise.'

Lily blushed. 'Of course you did. I knew that.' Determinedly stamping out the heat whipping through her, she pulled herself together and switched into business mode because, honestly, it was high time she stopped feeling like a giggly teenager in the grip of her first crush. 'I have a meeting across town. New client. Very big. Very important. Could be huge for us.' She glanced at her watch. 'In fact, I'd better get going.'

Filling with the familiar buzz she got whenever she pitched for new business, Lily stood up, grabbed her bag and hitched her handbag over her shoulder.

'Good luck,' said Zoe.

'Thanks.'

'Let me know how it goes.'

'I will.'

Sitting in a plush office in London's West End, Lily watched John Burrows, the director of marketing for what was going to be their most high-profile client to date, sign on the dotted line, and mentally punched the air in triumph.

It hadn't been an easy sale. He'd asked tough questions, demanded a lot of information and had driven an extremely hard bargain. At one point she'd thought her pitch had been about to unravel from the sheer pressure of it, but she'd held her nerve, conceded the points she was willing to concede and stood her ground on the ones she wasn't, and eventually they'd reached an agreement.

And now, she thought, smiling as he slid the document back for her to sign, she felt as if she were floating along in some kind of a fabulous narcotic-induced haze. Only she was high on adrenalin, success, life and love, not drugs. Her relationship was blooming, business was booming and frankly, she thought, adding her own signature beside his, it was pretty hard to see how things could get any better.

'We look forward to doing business with you,' she said, standing and holding out her hand with a smile.

John Burrows gave it a quick, firm shake and then let it go. 'Likewise.'

'Just out of interest,' she asked, putting the precious document away, 'how did you hear about us?'

'You were recommended.'

A wave of satisfaction and pride swept through her, tangling with everything else that was rolling around inside her and making it a pretty crowded place. Word of mouth was often the way they got clients, and it was good to know that they were still rated highly. 'Who by? If you don't mind saying.'

'I don't mind saying at all. It was Kit Buchanan.'

'Oh?' said Lily, her eyebrows lifting a little in surprise because Kit hadn't mentioned it. 'How do you know him?'

'I don't,' said John. 'But my wife does.'

'Really?' she asked with a smile. 'How?'

'Paula works with him. She does some of his PR from time to time. She asked him if he might know of anyone who might be able to help with what I was looking for and he suggested you.'

At the mention of PR in connection with Kit, Lily's blood chilled, all the good stuff draining away and leaving nothing but a hard, cold lump in her stomach. A tremor ran through her and her memory took her right back to the night he'd stumbled in in the early hours after that work night out and had confessed to having just slept with someone who'd worked in the PR department of the hotel where he was working.

A cold sweat broke out all over her skin and her throat

tightened and for a moment she went dizzy at the sickening thought that Kit still saw the woman he had a one-night stand with.

And then she gave herself a shake and got a grip. She was overreacting. Being absurd. Irrational. Seeing a co-incidence where it was highly unlikely that there was one because thousands of people worked in PR, and probably more than half of them were women.

Besides, if Kit had recommended *her* and they'd only been back together for a couple of months, then the chances were that Paula Burrows had only started working with Kit recently.

And finally, Kit would have told her if he actually now worked with the woman he'd cheated on her with, wouldn't he? Of course he would, because he'd promised her honesty and openness and had said he'd never give her any reason not to be able to trust him.

She believed him so she had nothing to worry about. Nothing to fear. She should give him the benefit of the doubt, attribute her bizarre reaction to John's news to her pathetic insecurities and leave it.

Lily left it for the ten minutes it took to wrap things up with her new client and walk to the lift and then the three she spent zooming down twenty-five storeys to the ground floor. She left it for the two minutes she needed to cross the lobby and walk out of the door, and the next two it took to cross the road and enter the garden square.

She left it, in fact, until she was sitting on a bench in the early spring sunshine, digging around in her handbag for her phone and inwardly cursing herself for being so piti-fully weak and insecure that she had to check out Paula Burrows for sure.

But what else could she do? she thought, finally locating her phone and hauling it out. For the last five of the seventeen minutes since the suspicion had taken root in her brain she'd been itching to do something about it because she'd realised somewhere between the fifteenth and fourteenth floors that in this case ignorance wasn't bliss. In this case ignorance was a bitch and she'd far rather be in possession of the facts, whatever they turned out to be.

After a couple of taps on the tiny screen of her smartphone Lily typed in 'Paula Burrows' along with 'PR' and the name of Kit's company.

And up she popped.

With her heart in her throat, Lily braced herself and scrolled through the woman's CV, bypassing the professional qualifications and industry awards until she got to the employment section.

The woman who might or might not have slept with her husband had had an impressive career so far. She'd been working for Kit's PR company for two years. Prior to that she'd worked at another top ten agency. And prior to *that* she'd worked in the PR department at the Brinkley Hotel Group. As had Kit. At the same time.

Which didn't automatically mean that they'd slept together, Lily told herself, frantically trying to cling onto logic as she fought not to hyperventilate, because presumably this Paula Burrows, or Barnes as she'd been then, hadn't been the only woman in the company's PR department.

But nor did it mean they hadn't, she thought, beginning to lose the battle with her breathing and logic. And if by horrible coincidence Kit did now work with the woman he'd had a one-night stand with and hadn't told her, what did it mean? What was going on?

She didn't know. A mere half an hour ago she'd been so certain about everything to do with her and Kit and their fabulous burgeoning relationship, but now with her head pounding with questions and doubts and her grip on her self-control rapidly disintegrating she suddenly didn't know anything any more.

All she did know was that she couldn't go back to the office and face Zoe's inevitable questions and relentless cheerfulness. Not while her thoughts were such a mess and the emotions she was struggling to keep in check were threatening to spill over.

So with a couple of taps and a quick swipe she found Zoe's number and hit the dial button.

'Hey,' came Zoe's cheerful voice down the line.

'Hi,' said Lily, her own voice sounding thick and croaky as if she hadn't used it in years.

'How did it go?'

'Good. We got it.'

'Great. Well done you. I'll put the champagne on ice.'

Lily lifted a hand to her pounding temple and closed her eyes because the last thing she felt like doing right now was celebrating. 'I think I might head home.'

There was a pause. 'Are you all right?'

'Fine. Just a bit of a headache, that's all.'

'Sure? You sound rough.'

'I feel it. But I'm sure I'll be fine in a bit.' Which was a lie because she couldn't imagine feeling fine any time soon.

'OK, well, try to rest.'

'I will.' Not.

'And I'll see you tomorrow.'

'See you tomorrow,' she echoed dully, and hung up.

In something of a daze she stumbled out of the park and hailed a taxi, and when it screeched to a halt gave the driver her address and climbed in.

She didn't notice much about the journey home. Her head was swirling too fast and her stomach was churning too violently.

What should she do about what she might or might not have just discovered? Should she confront Kit? Summon up her courage and ask him outright to clarify things? And whatever his response, should she bite the bullet and ask all those questions about the woman he'd betrayed her with that she'd been in too much of a state to ask at the time but had secretly wanted to ask for weeks—or years, if she was being honest?

Or should she just leave it?

Because she could well be getting the wrong end of the stick here. It could be a coincidence. He could have had the one-night stand with someone else in the PR department. And did she really want to bring the past up? Did she really want to know all the sordid details of what had happened five years ago? For what could possibly be no reason at all other than to satisfy her morbid curiosity?

No, she didn't, she thought firmly as the taxi pulled up outside her house and she got out, handed over a couple of notes and told the driver to keep the change. So she'd leave well alone. Put it to the back of her mind. Forget about it.

Things between her and Kit were good. Better than good. The searing—and probably wholly unnecessary—jealousy would fade. As would the hurt stabbing at her heart. With a bit of effort she could bury the doubt. And in a jiffy she would be back to normal.

Anyway, Kit was going away tomorrow and they had a lovely evening planned, and she wasn't going to rock this boat for anything.

CHAPTER ELEVEN

SOMETHING WAS UP, thought Kit, frowning to himself as he stood back to let Lily into the lift that would zoom them up to his suite. She'd been quiet throughout dinner. Pensive, monosyllabic and weirdly distant.

Given she'd just landed a huge deal, and considering she'd been aching to go to that restaurant since it had opened, her demeanour was unusual, disconcerting. He'd pulled strings and had managed to get a highly sought-after table at relatively short notice, and while he didn't need her gratitude a bit of enthusiasm would have been nice.

And not just about either the restaurant or the deal.

She'd been so excited when he asked her what she thought about moving in together, and so up for it, he'd found her excitement infectious. Earlier this evening, though, when he'd brought it up and made a joke about having to change the habit of a lifetime and start putting the lid back on the toothpaste she'd barely responded. Admittedly the joke hadn't exactly been side-splittingly hilarious but it hadn't even raised a roll of the eyes, and he found the change in her faintly disturbing.

So what was wrong? Was it something to do with work? Zoe? Him? And what was he going to do about it?

The doors swooshed open and as Lily went ahead of him into his open-plan living area, dropping her bag onto a chair and then shrugging out of her coat, for a moment he considered giving her time. Waiting until she sorted it out in her head and then either told him what was up or moved on.

And then he dismissed it.

No, he thought, setting his jaw and striding over to the cupboard in the kitchen that stocked the drinks. He'd made that mistake before and he wasn't making it again. He wouldn't give her the chance to avoid him. Wouldn't let her deflect. Whatever was wrong they could deal with it because so far things between them had been going brilliantly, and he wouldn't let them screw it up.

It was probably nothing more than a blip in any case, he told himself, pouring a whisky for himself and a glass of red for her. Nothing they couldn't sort out together if only she'd let him in.

He slid the glass of wine across the breakfast bar towards her and then leaned back against the counter and looked at her. 'OK, Lily, so what's up?'

She glanced up at him, her eyes weirdly empty, and despite the warmth of his apartment he felt a tiny shiver race down his spine. 'Nothing's up.'

Yeah, right. 'Is it work?'

'Why would anything be up at work?' she asked, knocking back almost half her wine.

Kit frowned because downing alcohol as if she needed the fortification wasn't like her. 'You tell me.'

'Work's fine.'

'Zoe, then?'

'She's fine too.'

That really only left one other option, because he might be many things but he wasn't stupid enough to ask if it was the time of the month, and that option was him.

He took a breath and braced himself. 'What have I done?'

'You? Nothing.'

'Right.'

She shrugged and drank what was left of her wine. 'Forget it. It's late and you have an early start. So let's go to bed.'

Feeling his patience begin to drain, Kit put his glass down and fought to stay calm. 'For goodness' sake, Lily. Don't do this. Didn't we say we'd communicate? Talk? Be open with each other? So tell me what's wrong. Whatever it is, I can take it.'

For a moment there was nothing but silence and as he waited for her to respond he became oddly aware of the beat of his heart, the tingling of his skin. An odd sense of impending doom seeped into him and for the first time since they'd got back together again he felt a flicker of panic.

Then she nodded. Once, briefly, and he didn't know if he was glad she agreed to open up or petrified at what she was going to say because there was an odd stillness about her. An eerie kind of control. The sort of calm that came before a storm.

'OK, fine,' she said, her voice so chilling and her small smile so horribly tight that he began to sweat. 'You're right. You're absolutely right.'

He felt himself tensing and a sudden rush of adrenalin, as if his body was preparing for something, although God knew what. 'So?'

'I have a question for you.'

'Go ahead.'

'Is Paula Burrows the woman you screwed while our marriage was in its death throes?'

As her words echoed through his apartment and shock rocked through him Kit went very still. Of all the possible issues that had been going through his head this hadn't been one of them so where the hell had this suddenly sprung from?

'How did you find out about Paula?' he said with a frown, and then winced because that was the wrong *wrong* way to put it. He'd made it sound as if Paula were a dirty little secret when nothing could be further from the truth. 'I mean, how did you hear about her?'

'My meeting today was with her husband,' she said, still alarmingly calm although a bit paler than she'd been a minute ago. 'He said you'd recommended us.'

'That's right. I did. I'd forgotten.'

'You'd forgotten?' she echoed in disbelief.

'It was a while ago.'

'And the answer to my question?'

Kit swallowed hard and killed the temptation to lie because even though it would be the easy way out of this he hadn't lied to her yet and he didn't intend to start now. He'd promised her honesty and she'd get it, whatever the fallout. 'The answer is yes,' he said, and waited for her reaction, not knowing how the hell he was going to handle it.

Lily went very pale and was gripping the stem of her glass so tightly her knuckles were white. 'I see,' she said with a faint nod. 'So let me get this straight. You work with the woman you cheated on me with. You still see her. And you didn't think to tell me.'

Knowing that if he wasn't careful this conversation could go very badly very easily, Kit decided to stick to the unvarnished truth, however brutal. 'It didn't occur to me,' he said, and inwardly winced because it might be the truth but it sounded wholly inadequate.

Lily stared at him as if unable to believe her ears. 'It didn't occur to you?'

'No. She's worked on a handful of projects for us and I've seen her at the most half a dozen times in the last couple of years.'

'And what do you do when you do? Reminisce about old times?'

'Of course not,' he said, choosing to ignore her sarcasm and remain calm and focused because in the face of her

evident anger that seemed the only way to get through this.
'It's just business.'

'But none of mine, it would seem.'

He heard the hurt and the bitterness in her voice and it
made his heart contract, but what could he say to that? The
truth was that he hadn't thought of Paula as the woman
he'd slept with since the morning after that terrible night,
when following his confession and the blazing row he'd
had with Lily he'd gone into work, resigned on the spot
and cleared his desk.

He hadn't thought to tell Lily about her because Paula
genuinely hadn't crossed his mind once in the last eight
weeks.

Now he wished he had. Now he wished he'd had time to
prepare for this because if he had he might have anticipated
Lily's anger and her hurt, he might have thought about her
insecurities and doubts and how they might make her respond to this kind of news and he might have formulated
a strategy to deal with it.

As it was he was navigating unfamiliar and extremely
choppy waters and he didn't have a clue what he was doing
and he now had the horribly panicky feeling that the longer
he said nothing, the worse things were becoming.

'Your silence speaks volumes, Kit,' said Lily with a bitter laugh as she apparently read his mind. 'And you know
what? You want communication? Well, this is the way I'm
choosing to communicate, you jerk.' And with that, she
hurled her glass at him.

With lightning reflexes Kit dodged to the left and the
glass flew over his right shoulder, smashed against a cupboard behind him and shattered, and the sound of it jolted
him out of paralysis.

She spun on her heel and marched off in the direction of
her coat and bag, but within a second he caught up with her,
grabbing her wrist and stopping her. She gasped in outrage

and he could feel her pulse jumping beneath his fingers but he ignored both as he whirled her round to face him.

'Let me go,' she said fiercely, trying to pull free.

Not a chance, he thought grimly, because whatever happened he wasn't letting her go ever again and they could get through this. They could. As long as he didn't mess it up. 'Why? So you can run away?'

'So I can leave before I do you some serious damage,' she said, her eyes flashing at him.

'That's a risk I'm prepared to take.'

'Fool.'

'Probably. But you don't get to run away from this this time.'

'Well, you don't get to decide what I do.'

That was true, but he did get to decide what *he* did, and if he wanted to fix this he had to start with the honesty and openness he'd promised her. 'Ask me about her, Lily,' he said. 'Ask me anything.'

Lily stopped struggling and stilled. Blinked a couple of times, and he thought he saw some of her hostility ebb. 'Anything?'

He relaxed his hold on her a fraction, but she didn't step back. 'Anything.'

'What makes you think I'm interested?'

'Aren't you?'

There was a moment's silence and he could virtually see the internal battle she was fighting. 'OK, fine,' she said, lifting her chin in challenge. 'What does this Paula person look like?'

'Average.'

She shook her head and glared at him. 'Not good enough, Kit. Not nearly good enough.'

'I mean it. Brown hair. Blue eyes. Around five foot six, I guess. Not fat. Not thin. Really average.'

'And what was she like in bed?' she asked bluntly. 'Better than me? Worse than me? Hotter? Kinkier? More adventurous? More creative? The woman is in PR after all.' She flashed him a look. 'And if you say "average" again I'll thump you.'

Kit ignored the thought that he really didn't want to be having this conversation because he didn't have a choice. Her questions and the insecurities they revealed were natural and justified and he wouldn't ignore them any more than he'd judge them. 'I don't remember.'

Lily rolled her eyes. 'Oh, please.'

'I really don't. I was hammered out of my skull.'

'Then why her?'

'Because she was there.' Inwardly he cringed as for the first time in years the memory of that night flashed into his head, but he didn't take his eyes off hers. 'I was at rock-bottom and she was there.'

'Such a charmer.'

'You wanted honesty, you have it. I'm not proud of what I did, Lily.'

'Does she know you were using her?'

'Yes.'

'You told her?'

'We had a chat the first time she turned up at a project meeting.'

'Cosy.'

'Not particularly. It was awkward.'

'My heart bleeds.'

'Nothing's happened, Lily. Not since that night. And it won't. It was a mistake and we both are more than aware of that. If that doesn't convince you then how about the fact that I'm with you and she's married?'

'So what? That didn't stop *you*.'

'Happily.'

Lily flinched. 'You know her well enough to know that, do you?'

'I asked. We chatted. I apologised. She forgave me. We've moved on.'

He'd thought Lily had forgiven him too because hadn't she said she had way back when they'd first talked? But that clearly wasn't the case, and he'd been a fool not to see it.

He'd thought that their relationship had been going well, but the progress he'd naively assumed they'd made had been nothing more than superficial. Physically things couldn't be better. Emotionally, however, they were still rocky in a way he hadn't appreciated. But now he could see that beneath the surface there'd been an undercurrent of mistrust, and why wouldn't there be because, as he was beginning to realise, he wasn't the only one who had to constantly live with the knowledge of what he'd done.

And he might have nothing to feel guilty about, nothing to be ashamed of this time, but that didn't matter. It was because of what he'd done that Lily was feeling so insecure and hurt and if he wanted to hang on to her he was going to have to do a lot more than simply be open and honest. He was going to have to prove to her that she could trust him and how he was going to do that he had no idea.

Hell, if only he didn't have to go to Rome tomorrow, because he could really do with the time and headspace to think about this properly.

'I thought I had too,' said Lily quietly. 'But it seems I might not be as over all this as I'd thought.'

Kit felt his chest tighten. 'Is it a deal-breaker?'

She shrugged and sighed. 'I don't know.'

'Is there anything I can do to make it right?'

She looked up at him for a couple of long minutes, as if searching his face and eyes for sincerity, bit her lip and then frowned. 'You really want to make it right?' she said, her frown clearing as she pulled her shoulders back and lifted her chin in a way that had wariness trickling through him.

'Of course.'

'Then use another PR agency.'

As her ultimatum sank in Kit went still, his mind reeling and his heart sinking as he realised he'd been right to be wary because of all the things she could have asked of him she'd asked for the one thing he couldn't give her.

He got that this was some kind of test. He got that she wanted him to prove that he meant what he said. And he'd have done just about anything. But firing his PR agency? That he couldn't do. There was no way he was going to let something personal ruin a perfectly good business relationship. Certainly not one that had taken years to build up and now worked brilliantly for both parties.

'I can't do that, Lily.'

She stared up at him in disbelief. 'I thought you wanted to make this right?'

'I do. But not like that.'

'Why not?'

'Because they're the best in the business and we have an excellent relationship. And I can't let something personal get in the way of that.'

'OK, fine,' she said, with a small smile he didn't like one little bit. 'Then ask Paula to resign or switch to a different team or something.'

His heart sank further. 'I can't do that either.'

'Why not?'

'Because she's very good at her job and it would be grossly unfair. If not downright illegal.'

'I see,' she said coolly, but he didn't think she did. 'So you really won't fire them or get rid of her?'

'I won't.'

Lily pushed against his chest and took a step back. 'Then I really don't think there's anything else to be said, do you?'

CHAPTER TWELVE

THE FOLLOWING MORNING Lily stumbled in to work, late for the first time since she and Zoe had begun working together, but that wasn't hugely surprising since she'd only fallen asleep at dawn. She was feeling on edge and cranky and not just from lack of sleep.

'Morning,' said Zoe, looking up from her monitor and shooting her a smile. 'At last. I was beginning to worry.'

'Sorry.' Lily dumped her bag on her desk with rather more force than was necessary and then stalked over to the coffee machine.

'How are you feeling? Headache better?'

'What?' she muttered, stuffing an espresso capsule into the top and slamming the lid shut.

'Your headache,' said Zoe again, only a little slower. 'Is it better?'

'No.' Her head hurt like hell, but then it would given the half a bottle of wine she'd polished off when she'd got home last night.

'Are you sure you should be here, Lily?' said Zoe, concern evident in her voice. 'You look absolutely awful.'

'Gee, thanks,' said Lily, grabbing a cup, sticking it beneath the spout and pressing the button while thinking that however awful she looked it wasn't a patch on how awful she felt.

Last night, that scene with Kit, had been horrible, she

reflected with a shudder. So much for hoping that the unnecessary—she'd thought—jealousy would fade. And so much for being able to ignore the doubts she'd had in that garden square. All afternoon while she'd been sitting at home alone with her thoughts and practically climbing the walls, the jealousy and doubts had been growing, feeding rapaciously off her insecurities and her fears.

But she'd made herself calm down and by the time she'd joined Kit for dinner she'd thought she could contain the swell of emotion. Control it. Ignore it. Clearly she'd been mistaken because he'd pushed and prodded and poked until she hadn't been able to take any more and she'd exploded.

Right up until the point where he'd confirmed what she'd suspected she'd been willing to give him the benefit of the doubt. She'd totally been prepared to accept that she'd indulged her penchant for melodrama and overreacted.

In her heart of hearts she hadn't expected him to admit she was right. Deep down she'd hoped he'd deny it. Tell her she was being an idiot, that the coincidence was just that.

But when he'd confirmed it, well, that had been just awful. That had made a mockery of all the silken promises he'd given her on the island. The promises of the last two months. All that nonsense about honesty and openness and communication when he'd been lying to her from the very moment he'd barged his way back into her life. Or at the very least lying by omission and not telling her something he should have realised she'd want to know.

Once she'd got over the shock of it she'd been so, *so* angry. So deeply hurt and fiercely disappointed and so rocked by the realisation that despite what she'd told him, despite what she'd thought, she evidently hadn't forgiven him for what he'd done, she'd lost control. And that was why she'd done what she'd done and said what she'd said.

Back at home and in bed, her head churning, she'd hardly slept a wink. With time and distance in which to think more objectively than she'd been able to at the time, and with the anger and hurt fading, she'd found herself hating the way she and Kit had argued, wishing she'd held back, wishing she'd been under better control, wishing she hadn't let her emotions get the better of her. Above all she wished she hadn't given into the need to test his commitment to them by issuing that awful, hugely unfair ultimatum.

'No, seriously, Lily,' said Zoe worriedly, 'you don't look well at all.'

'I'm fine.'

'No, you're not. What's happened?'

'I'm hung-over, that's all.'

'Big night?'

'You could say that.'

'How was the restaurant?'

'The restaurant was fine.' The food had been divine. The atmosphere, however, had been positively frosty and things had gone downhill from there.

'And how's Kit?' asked her sister, zeroing in on the trouble with a precision born from experience.

'I haven't a clue.'

'What happened?'

'The honeymoon's over.' She wasn't sure the whole thing wasn't over and her heart actually physically hurt at the thought.

There was a pause while Zoe absorbed this news. 'Huh?'

'We had a row.'

'About what?'

The machine having done its job, Lily lifted the cup and took it back to her desk. 'Remember the one-night stand he had?' she said, sitting down and wrapping her hands round it as if the heat might give her the strength to relive the horrors of last night's scene.

'How could I forget?'

'It turns out she works with him.'

Zoe's jaw dropped and her eyebrows shot up. 'No,' she breathed.

'Yes.'

Taking advantage of her sister's astonishment and speechlessness Lily sipped her coffee and filled her in on the details of how she'd found out.

'What did you do?' said Zoe, once Lily had finished her rundown.

'Lost it.'

'I'm not surprised.'

'I threw a wine glass at him.'

Zoe winced. 'Full?'

'Empty.'

'Classy.'

'I know,' said Lily with a sigh. 'Not exactly my finest moment.'

'I'd say you had provocation, and look on the bright side—it could have been worse.'

'How?'

'You could have taken a key to his car, scissors to his suits and emailed his backers.'

'There is that,' said Lily with a grimace. 'And at least I didn't bottle it all up as usual.'

'You certainly didn't.' Zoe shook her head. 'But, Lil, that ultimatum… Really?'

'I know,' said Lily glumly. 'It was wholly unreasonable. Grossly unfair. I shouldn't have done it. I'm mortified that I did, but I wasn't exactly thinking clearly.'

'So what happens now? Are the two of you over?'

She'd asked herself the same thing all through the night, but still didn't have an answer. 'I don't know,' she said, filling with a deep ache. 'I hope not because I know I overreacted and that it was a heat-of-the-moment kind of thing. Paula Burrows isn't the problem. Kit and I are. Me in particular.'

'Has he called?'

Lily shook her head a bit too vigorously, and despite the coffee her head started pounding again. 'No. And I'm not sure he will.'

'Why on earth not?'

'I think I owe him an apology,' she said, rubbing her temples and grimacing.

'It sounds like he owes you one too.'

'Possibly.'

'So what's stopping you from calling him?'

'He's in Rome.'

'And?'

'It's not the sort of conversation I want to have over the phone. There may be grovelling. From me at least. And it's not going to be pretty.'

Zoe shot her a smile. 'In that case,' she said, 'don't you think the phone sounds rather perfect?'

Zoe was right, thought Lily as she unlocked her front door after getting home from work and went inside. What was wrong with apologising and possibly grovelling over the phone? Nothing. Her blushes, and Kit's, would be spared, and actually it was the only option she had because frankly she didn't think her nerves could stand another night like last night.

She dumped her bag on the floor and hung her coat up and glanced at her watch. In fact she'd do it right now. Strike while the iron was hot and all that. It was seven o'clock, eight in Rome. Too late for a meeting or a site visit, surely. Kit would be having supper. A drink. Working in his hotel room, perhaps.

Maybe even waiting to hear from her.

Brightening a bit at that, she went into the kitchen and poured herself some wine—her hangover having been taken care of earlier by three more espressos and two bags of crisps—then picked up her phone.

Tapping it against her mouth, she wandered into the sitting room and settled herself on the sofa. Right. So. What was she going to say? And how was she going to say it?

Ten minutes later, Lily had a strategy of sorts and a few points jotted down so that she didn't forget them, and she was more than ready to apologise, grovel and do whatever else Kit asked of her. She also had an empty glass of wine and cheeks red with embarrassment at the memory of how she'd behaved last night but that was fine because he wasn't going to get to see either.

With her heart in her mouth she picked up the phone and dialled his mobile. Which went straight through to voice-mail without ringing. She hung up. Tried again. But the same thing happened so she left a message asking him to call her when he had a chance. And then texted.

Trying to keep a lid on a simmering sense of frustration next she tried the hotel he'd told her he was staying at. But there was no answer from his room there either, and the reception desk couldn't help.

Out of ideas, Lily put the phone on the coffee table. Then sat back and frowned as she felt herself sort of deflate. She'd made notes, dammit. Thought about this at length and in detail. She'd also summoned up quite a lot of her courage to call, and after such a build-up the let-down was huge. She felt oddly cheated. And just the teensiest bit put out because after all the lengths—the emotional ones especially—she'd gone to to contact him, the least he could do was be there to listen to what she had to say.

So where was he? Who was he with? What was he doing? And should she be worried?

Of course she shouldn't be worried, she told herself sternly. He was probably out. Or in the shower. The bat tery of his mobile might be flat. Or he might be somewhere where he didn't get a signal.

On the other hand, their argument last night had been pretty hum-dinging, and she had been kind of unreasonable and irrational, so could she have driven him into the arms of another woman? Someone comforting and amenable, not argumentative and melodramatic.

Lily went cold and her heart slowed right down as her head swam at the thought of Kit with someone else. And then she blinked, gave herself a quick shake and pulled herself together. No. She was being ridiculous. That wasn't at all likely.

Was it?

No. No. No.

They'd had one argument. Big deal. Millions of couples across the globe did. All the time. More often probably. It was normal. Nothing to worry about. She just needed to relax, that was all. Get a sense of perspective. Not leap to wholly unlikely conclusions based on her massive insecurities.

There was bound to be a perfectly rational explanation for why Kit wasn't answering his phone. Absolutely bound to be.

Stifling a yawn because now that he was done for the day the exhaustion he'd been holding at bay since he'd got up this morning was pouring through him like a tidal wave, Kit climbed the steps from the basement restaurant where he'd had dinner and then left his colleagues ordering more drinks, and checked his phone.

Two missed calls. One message. One text. All from Lily.

The desire to call her had been needling him all day. He'd felt the urge to talk to her hammering away in the back of his mind throughout the site visit and the meetings that had taken up the rest of the day. But he'd been unable to do either because he'd barely had a moment to himself to think, let alone work out what he wanted to say to her and how to say it.

Now he did, but it was late. Nearly midnight here and therefore eleven in London. He ought not to disturb her. He ought to wait until morning. On the other hand he didn't think he could stand another night like last night during which his conscience had niggled at him so relentlessly that he'd hardly slept.

What the hell? he thought, tapping the reply button to her text message and typing Too late to call? Nothing ventured, nothing gained.

Then he hailed a passing taxi, and, after it pulled to a screeching halt beside him, climbed in and gave the driver the address of his hotel in his very dodgy Italian. As he sat back and rubbed a hand over his eyes, his phone beeped and he sat up, more alert than he'd felt at any other moment today.

Never was Lily's reply, and within a second he was dialling her number, his heart lurching in a way that had nothing to do with the driver, who clearly thought he was at Monza.

The phone had barely rung before she picked up. 'Hi,' she said, sounding breathy, as if she'd had to run for the phone, which she couldn't have if she'd only texted seconds ago.

'Hi,' said Kit. 'Sorry it's so late. I've only just picked up your messages. I was out for dinner with a couple of people from work. A basement place. No signal.'

He heard her let out a breath and when she spoke again she sounded strangely relieved. 'That's OK. How's it been going?'

'Fine. Good.'

'Good.' There was a moment's silence and Kit was just about to fill it when Lily got there first. 'Look, Kit,' she said, her voice soft and husky and sending a stab of desire shooting through him. 'I'm so sorry about last night.'

Kit nearly dropped the phone. *She* was sorry? 'If anyone should be apologising, Lily, it's me.'

'Whatever for? I was the one who called you a jerk and threw a glass at you. I'm the one who hurled that ultimatum at you, which was utterly unforgivable. Of course I don't expect you to fire your PR agency. I'm sorry I suggested it, and if it's any consolation I'm mortified.'

'You had justification to be angry,' he muttered, not entirely happy about the fact that she thought she was in the wrong. 'I should have told you about Paula. And if it had ever crossed my mind I would have. I never think of her outside the context of her working for me. She genuinely means nothing to me. Please believe me on this.'

Lily sighed. 'I do. I think. And with hindsight I'm not sure that last night was really about her.'

He frowned in the darkness. 'It wasn't?'

'No. Because I've thought about it, and, you know, I *do* forgive you.'

'Then what was it about?'

'I had a little wobble, that's all. Freaked out for a moment.'

'Over us?'

'Maybe.'

'Why?'

There was a brief moment of silence and Kit could imagine her frowning, biting her lip as she worked it out. 'I think I'm a bit scared, Kit. This has all been so fast. It's kind of overwhelming.'

'There's nothing to be scared of, sweetheart.'

'There's me. And then there's this all going wrong and my life falling apart again. Last time I eventually put myself back together again but if everything goes wrong this time I'd be in bits, and the really terrifying thing is that I'm not sure that I'd be able to put myself back together.'

'You won't have to because it won't happen.'

'How can you know that?'

'Because this time whenever you're scared or vulnerable, or whenever you think something's overwhelming you, tell me and I'll be there.'

'I wish you were here now,' she said quietly.

'So do I. But I'll be back tomorrow morning and we can spend the rest of the weekend making up.'

'I can't wait.' For a moment neither of them spoke. Then she said, 'Kit?'

'What?'

'I love you.'

'I love you too, sweet pea. Deeply. I always have, always will. Even when you're throwing glasses at me and issuing unreasonable ultimatums.'

'So are we OK?'

The faint tremor in her voice cut him to the quick and at that moment he knew that he'd do everything in his power to make sure of it. 'Of course we are.'

CHAPTER THIRTEEN

But they weren't OK. At least Lily wasn't.

At first she'd clutched onto Kit's reassurance that they were fine as if it were a lifeline, and had buried the tiny bubble of doubt somewhere deep inside where it wouldn't bother her.

Which hadn't been all that hard because when he'd got back from Rome everything had been so lovely. After a weekend spent making up as promised, he'd announced that he was going to cut back on work and delegate as much as he could. With the extra time, if she was amenable to the idea, he was going to woo her.

Lily had been very amenable to the idea, and had adored the dates, the dinners and the two minibreaks he'd taken her on. He'd poured every drop of spare energy into them and she'd fallen more and more in love with him every day that had passed.

Which made the fact that the doubt she tried to get rid of kept bubbling away all the more frustrating.

And she did try. Really hard. She tried to focus on the present, on the relationship she and Kit had now and the many, many positives of that. She told herself not to look too far into the future and simply to take one day at a time, as he'd suggested all those weeks ago when they'd been on that island.

But to her despair she kept slipping back into the past.

She kept dwelling on the latter stages of their marriage and reliving all the pain and hurt that she'd suffered.

She didn't know why she did it. She certainly didn't want to. Most of the time she wanted to reach right inside her head and yank out all the thoughts and doubts and fears churning around inside. But she couldn't seem to help it.

Just as she couldn't seem to help the horrible, insidious, burning desire to check Kit's phone whenever he left it un-attended. Or the almost irresistible temptation to casually open up his inbox and take a look at his emails whenever he was away from his laptop. Especially after the rare occasion he hadn't been able to delegate and had had to go away.

She hated it. Hated the way suspicion was slowly creeping into everything she did and everything she felt when it came to Kit. She hated the fact that she knew it was happening yet couldn't seem to stop it however much she told herself that they were fine, that things were going great.

Because the truth was things weren't going so great and it was all her fault. As she'd dreaded, she was handling the things that were going on in her head and in her heart really badly. Most of the time she wasn't handling them at all.

Kit was trying his best. In addition to the attention he lavished on her and the way he kept her up to date of everything he was doing and everyone he was seeing he kept sitting her down and asking her what was wrong, telling her that he wasn't going anywhere so she might as well spit it out. But she had the feeling they could have spent a week in the same room with him endlessly attempting to get her to talk and still she wouldn't have been able to explain.

She didn't know what was wrong. She didn't know how much longer she could stand the emotional distance that was beginning to stretch between the two of them. Didn't know what to do about it. Didn't know what would happen if she confronted it. Didn't want to think about what it might mean for them.

From time to time she caught him looking at her. Worriedly, sadly, frequently frustratedly, and she couldn't blame him because the expression in his eyes reflected how she felt. Their relationship was slowly imploding and she couldn't seem to do a thing to stop it, and it was breaking her heart.

By the time Zoe's hen night came around, Lily was so low, so confused and so adrift that she really wasn't in the mood for partying. But what could she do? She wasn't going to back out. What with Zoe's practically non-existent circle of friends, she and Dan's sister, Celia, were the only guests, and she wasn't going to dampen her sister's happiness with her doubts and unhappiness.

So as the trio walked down the stairs into the basement lounge bar in Notting Hill, Lily plastered on a smile, and when the waitress asked what they'd like to drink she ordered a margarita.

Then another.

And another.

And then she started enjoying herself.

Zoe was sparkling like the diamond solitaire that adorned the third finger of her left hand. Celia was wickedly clever and outrageously entertaining. The place was jumping, the tapas-style food delicious and she had a nice buzz. Almost nice enough to forget what a hash she was making of things with Kit.

'Right,' said Celia, once the waitress had returned with a fresh round of drinks. 'So I know this is Zoe's hen night and everything, but to be honest, as that *Mr & Mrs* quiz thing proved, she's so besotted by my brother that that story's boring.'

'Hey,' protested Zoe.

'Well, it is.' With a grin Celia turned to Lily. 'Your relationship on the other hand sounds absolutely fascinating.'

Lily somehow managed to drum up a smile, but it was

hard when despite the uplifting effect of the tequila her spirits plummeted. 'Fascinating is not the word,' she said dully.

'Then what is? Awesome? Steaming? Mind-blowing?'

'Technically mind-blowing's two words,' said Zoe.

'The word you're looking for is hopeless,' said Lily, and to her horror she could feel the backs of her eyes beginning to prickle.

Celia stared at her. 'What?'

'Mine's a study in how not to have a relationship,' she said, the happy buzz now a dim and distant memory as the desolation and loneliness she'd been feeling recently welled up inside her.

'Oh? How come?'

Lily swallowed. 'First time round we screwed it up so badly I shut myself off and Kit had a one-night stand.'

In the ensuing silence Celia stared at her. 'Jeez.'

'I know,' said Zoe. 'Bad, huh?'

Celia frowned. 'But now you're back together.'

Lily nodded and sighed. 'Yes. And making a complete and utter hash of it.'

Zoe gasped. Celia simply shook her head in amazement. 'I'm not surprised, because, really, how could you ever trust him after something like that?'

And just like that Lily froze as the truth of it struck her. Celia had hit the nail on the head. She didn't trust him. At all. 'I can't,' she breathed and, as the knowledge sank in, felt as if a great weight had been lifted from her because suddenly all the confusion and questions she'd been tormenting herself with recently made sense. Absolute and devastating sense.

'What?' said Zoe, looking at her worryingly.

'I don't trust him,' she said, faintly reeling. 'I don't think I have for months.'

'Oops,' muttered Celia. 'I really shouldn't have asked.'

For a split second Lily was tempted to agree with her because part of her would rather have remained in the dark.

Now she knew, though, she had no choice but to admit what she'd probably known every time she'd had to stop herself reaching for his phone or laptop. Every time he'd gone out or away and the niggle of doubt over what he was really doing and who he was really with had returned. Every time she'd secretly wondered whether he was telling her the truth.

Everything that logic would have told her had she not been so deeply in denial.

She didn't trust him.

Her mind spun with the thought of it, the thought of what it meant, which was now blindingly, agonisingly clear. There was only one way for their relationship to go, she realised as her heart wrenched, because she might love him with everything she was and everything she had, but that didn't mean anything without trust.

She had to talk to him. Had to explain. Even if it meant the end. She owed him the truth, however heartbreaking it was going to be, and she owed it to him now.

'Zoe, Celia, I'm sorry,' she said, now feeling as sober as if she'd been drinking nothing but water all night as she got shakily to her feet, her eyes stinging and her throat tight, 'but I've got to go.'

Kit was sitting in the dark in the garden with a half-empty bottle of whisky and a glass when he heard the front door slam.

When Lily had gone out he'd initially been in what was now his study, kidding himself that he was working, much as he'd done every day lately.

But that was a joke, wasn't it, because how could he concentrate on work when his life with Lily was slowly disintegrating? How could he think about anything other than the fact that it was happening again? That Lily was slipping away from him like water through fingers and, once again, he didn't know what the hell to do about it.

He could feel that he was losing her and it scared him witless. Made him ache and filled his heart with pain.

Because he'd tried. So hard. Alone in his room that night in Rome he'd figured out his priorities and had basically changed his entire life for her. He'd decided to put her first, work second and to set about winning her back.

So with the focus and dedication that had built him a successful hotel business in five short years he'd wined and dined her. Reminded her of the man she'd fallen in love with and shown her the better man he'd become. He'd shared with her every detail of what he was doing and who he was with when he wasn't with her. He'd stripped his soul bare for her, told her things he'd never told anyone and trusted her with everything he was.

But it wasn't enough.

Time and time again he'd asked Lily what was wrong, and time and time again she'd looked at him, said she didn't know. He didn't think she was lying. She seemed so genuinely tormented by the question every time he asked that he got the impression that she was as much at a loss to understand what was happening as he was. And, unlike the night they'd argued about Paula, pushing her for an answer wasn't going to work.

He didn't know what would work. All he knew was that she wasn't happy and it was just about killing him.

But what had gone wrong? he wondered, frowning out into the quiet still of the night as for about the billionth time he tried to work it out. He'd thought they'd reached a deeper level of understanding. That this time their relationship was on firmer emotional ground, but maybe he was wrong because over the weeks she'd become increasingly

subdued. More watchful and wary somehow. She'd withdrawn into herself, just as she'd done before.

Maybe he'd pushed her too hard, he thought. Maybe
moving in together so soon had been a mistake. Maybe she
hadn't changed in the way he'd thought—hoped—she had.

Maybe they simply weren't meant to be together.

At the thought of that Kit felt his stomach turn inside out
and something deep inside him begin to ache. And then he
set his jaw and pulled himself together. No. That was rubbish. They *were* meant to be together. All he had to do was
think of a way to fix this because what they were going
through wasn't insurmountable. It couldn't be.

Behind him a light went on inside and as he heard Lily
step out onto the terrace, the trace of her scent drifting
towards him and every one of his senses zooming in on
her, just as they always did, his heart began to thud with
renewed resolve because the solution would come to him.
Eventually. It had to.

'What are you doing out here?' she said softly.

'Thinking.'

'About what?'

How he could make things between them right. 'Nothing much.'

She moved round into his line of sight and his heart
lurched crazily the way it did every time he saw her.

But tonight something was different. It wasn't the lack
of a smile on her lovely face or the absence of the sparkle
in her beautiful eyes because he'd got used to both. It was
something about the way she held herself, something in
the deadness of her expression, something that made him
go icy-cold.

As a ribbon of apprehension and dread wound itself
round his insides he felt something inside him wither and
all he could think was that somehow it was too late. Some-

how they'd got to a point where things couldn't be fixed and he hadn't noticed soon enough.

'You're back early,' he said, swallowing back the sudden lump in his throat.

'Yes.'

'Not much fun?'

'Not a lot.'

She sat down next to him, turned to face him, and Kit wished he could turn back time and not be here when she got back because he didn't want this now. He didn't want this at all. Yet on some dim and distant level he knew it had been a long time coming. Knew it was inevitable. Wished he'd had time to prepare his arguments, wished he had arguments to prepare.

'Want a drink?' he said.

'No, thanks.'

'Mind if I have one?'

'Go ahead.'

He poured himself another glass of whisky and noticed his hand was shaking. 'You're going to say we need to talk, aren't you?'

A flicker of surprise flashed in her eyes and then she nodded. 'Yes.'

'Because this isn't working, is it?' he said, the struggle he was having keeping a grip on his emotions making his voice hoarse.

'No.'

'Want to tell me why?'

Her eyes filled with tears and her chin trembled and it was all he could do not to take her in his arms and tell her everything was going to be all right because he didn't think it was. 'I can't bear to.'

'Tell me, Lily. I won't break.' Although the possibility was there.

'But I might.'

'Come on,' he said, trying to give her a smile but failing. 'Be brave.'

She nodded and blinked, but it didn't get rid of the shimmer of tears and it didn't stop the tremble of her chin. 'I thought I could do this,' she said, her voice breaking. 'But I can't.'

'Why not?'

'Because there's this thing.' She rubbed her chest and frowned as if she didn't totally get it. 'It's so tiny. But it's there. And I just can't seem to get rid of it. That night you went away the first time, after we had that argument about Paula, I couldn't get hold of you and I couldn't help wondering what you were doing and who you were with.'

'I told you what I was doing and who I was with.'

'I know. And I believed you. I still do. But I think it started something and it won't go back.'

'What is it?'

'A lack of trust.'

'You can trust me.'

'Can I?'

'Of course you can.'

'But how do I know that? Tell me, because I desperately want to.'

She looked at him despairingly, as if it was something she'd asked herself a dozen times over, and what could he say? Because she could? What kind of an answer was that? Apart from the only one he had. He'd never do anything to betray her trust, but how could he expect her to believe him when he'd already broken it once?

'Because I love you.'

She put a hand on his cheek and he could feel his skin burning beneath her touch. 'And I love you. More than I ever did before. At the risk of sounding soppy you are my sun and stars. You're the only man I've ever wanted. The only man I've ever loved and probably ever will love. The thought of never kissing you again, never holding you again or never speaking to you again makes me feel physically sick. I have this pain deep inside me, like a hand's reaching right inside and twisting everything inside me into knots.'

'Then don't think about it.'

'I have to.'

'Why?'

'Because without trust loving you isn't enough.' She shook her head and pulled her hand away and the loss of her warmth felt like an icicle through his heart. 'It's not going to work, Kit. It's just not going to work.'

At the sad finality in her voice panic welled up inside him. 'What can I do, Lily? Tell me. Whatever it is I'll do it.'

'There's nothing either of us can do.'

'There must be.'

'There isn't.'

And it was all his fault, he knew. He'd done this to them the minute he'd destroyed her ability to trust him by cheating on her and Kit felt the knowledge hit him as if someone had thumped him in the solar plexus. He didn't deserve her love. He didn't deserve her trust. He wasn't worthy of her. And he had to let her go. 'Lily…'

'I know. I'm sorry,' she whispered, the tears now flowing down her cheeks as she leaned forwards and gently kissed him. 'So sorry.'

He kissed her back, knowing that it was a kiss goodbye, and it just about broke him apart. 'So am I, my darling,' he said. 'So am I.'

CHAPTER FOURTEEN

ON A PROFESSIONAL level the last fortnight had been great for Kit. Plans for the new hotel in Rome were coming along apace and business was booming. To his delight—and no small amount of relief—Paula Burrows had been head-hunted by another PR firm and just yesterday he'd heard that one of his hotels was up for an award.

On a personal level, however, the last couple of weeks had been diabolical. However busy he kept himself, however hard he worked, he couldn't stop thinking about Lily. He couldn't stop wondering how she was and what she was doing, and he'd been going mad wondering if there was anything during their relationship that he could have done differently.

He couldn't seem to get rid of the dull ache that lived deep inside him, the pain that filled every cell of his body or the sorrow and regret that washed over him practically every other minute.

The need to find out how she was drummed through him constantly and the temptation to call her had been so hard to resist that he'd had to delete her details from his phone.

If only it had been as easy to delete her from his memory. But that was nigh on impossible because she was in there all the time. Teasing him. Tormenting him. Driving him pretty much insane.

And making him do all kinds of things he'd really rather

not do. Such as getting up in the early hours and searching the web for news, photos or anything really that might give him a hit of her. Such as composing emails he'd never ever send. Such as on one particularly bad night driving round to her house, parking up outside and waiting for the merest glimpse of her.

It had to stop, thought Kit, rubbing his hand along his stubbly jaw and then across the back of his neck as he sat in his kitchen and brooded. It really did. Quite apart from the fact that some of the things he'd done lately bordered on stalkerish, as painful as it was, as much as his heart was aching, Lily had made it very clear that they were over, and he knew perfectly well that there wasn't a thing he could do about it.

Hadn't he tried during the entire time they'd been together? And then the night in her garden, hadn't he abandoned his pride? Hadn't he begged? Hadn't he very nearly wept, for goodness' sake?

Well, he wouldn't be doing any of that again, he thought with a shudder at the memory of how desperate to hold on to her he'd been and the lengths he'd gone to to achieve it. And he wouldn't be doing any of the other things he resorted to in his wretchedness any more. He'd had enough of the heartache and he was pretty sure that his staff had had enough of his filthy mood. So there'd be no more web searching. No more seeking her out. No more thinking about her. And after this lunchtime, no more playing squash with Dan just so he could pump him for information.

He had to excise her from his memory and his heart because he didn't deserve her and he couldn't have her and he might as well get used to the idea.

Lily stood on the dais in the fitting room of the bridal shop, risked a quick glance in the mirror directly in front of her and practically recoiled in horror at her reflection. She looked absolutely hideous.

When she'd dragged herself out of bed this morning after yet another night of too many tears and too little sleep she'd slapped on some make-up and hauled a brush through her hair and thought she wasn't doing too badly considering how wretched she felt.

But under the harsh bright fluorescent light of the fitting room she saw that she'd been deluding herself. Great grey bags sagged beneath her eyes. There were hollows beneath her cheekbones. Her hair hung limply and dully around her ears, and despite the tinted moisturiser she'd applied—very patchily it seemed—her skin was the colour of wallpaper paste.

Whichever way she looked at it, and given the many mirrors surrounding her that was a lot, she wasn't doing the gorgeous floaty silk dress she was wearing any kind of justice.

But was it any wonder?

The last time that she and Kit had broken up everyone had said that she'd get over it. That all she needed was time. And while she'd been miserable they'd been proved right. But that strategy wasn't working so well for her now and, as she'd feared, it didn't look as if there was any hope that it would.

It had been a fortnight since he'd prised her off him and walked out of her garden, her house and her life, and she was no better now than she had been then. If anything she was worse because she was finding it pretty impossible to see how she was ever going to get over him.

She thought about him constantly. Dreamed about him regularly. Every morning when she woke up she remembered that they were over, and her heart shattered all over again.

Most of Kit's stuff had been gone for days now—

he'd been round when she'd been at work, packed up and dropped the key through the letter box—but every now and then she found something he'd forgotten. A random sock that had made it into her drawer. His toothbrush lying beside the basin. A copy of the *Financial Times* folded in the way that only he folded it. And every single time she'd come across something of his—or even something that merely reminded her of him—she crumpled into a heap on the floor in a flood of tears.

This wasn't like the last time when every time he'd crossed her mind she'd mainly thought 'good riddance' and 'what a relief'. This was hell on earth. Absolute agony. Because, as a result of all their baggage and the way they'd managed to deal with most of it, their relationship this time round had been deeper than before. Closer. And thus the break-up was all the more devastating.

Ending things might have been the only thing she could have done after discovering that she might love him to bits but she just couldn't trust him, but that didn't make it easier to bear. It didn't lessen the pain and didn't make her miss him any less.

This time she knew there'd be no third chance. No trying again. This time, this really was it.

As the reality of what she'd done slammed into her head yet again, Lily could feel the tears welling up again and she sniffed them back because she really couldn't damage this dress. She'd never forgive herself. Neither would Zoe, who'd been sitting on the sofa while the seamstress had rotated round Lily sticking pins into the fabric. Zoe, who was also proving surprisingly unsympathetic about her sister's miserable, agonising plight.

Now the seamstress, having finished her alterations, helped Lily out of the dress and carried it off, leaving Lily to step down off the dais and pull on her clothes aware that her sister was watching her every move.

'What?' she muttered, unable to bear the scrutiny a second longer as she did up her jeans and made a mental note to buy a belt.

'When did you last eat?'

Eat? Had she had a piece of toast last night perhaps? She couldn't remember. 'A while ago,' she said.

'Fancy some lunch?' said Zoe.

Nearly throwing up at the idea of lunch, Lily swallowed back the wave of nausea and shrugged her jacket on. 'Thanks, but I don't think I could stomach lunch right now.'

'Then you can watch me eat.'

'Not sure I want to do that either.'

'Too bad,' said Zoe, taking her arm in a surprisingly firm grip and marching her out of the shop, 'because I'm hungry and we need to have a little chat.'

Five minutes later, Zoe, with a determination Lily would never have expected from her previously non-confrontational sister, had found a pub, ordered two plates of fish and chips and two glasses of white wine and had plonked her down at a table in the corner.

'Right,' said Zoe, effectively blocking her escape by sitting down opposite her and then giving her an oddly fierce glare. 'This has gone on long enough.'

'What has?'

'You. The long face. The wallowing.'

Lily stared at her sister. What the hell? 'I'm allowed to wallow,' she said as her heart gave a great squeeze. 'Kit and I broke up. I'm devastated.'

'Well, get over it, because I'm not having you lose any more weight. This is the second time your dress has had to be taken in in a week. Carry on at this rate and there'll be nothing left of you.'

'Thanks for the sympathy, bridezilla. And come to think of it, where is that anyway?'

'Where's what?'

'The sympathy. You're supposed to be mopping me up the way I mopped you up when Dan ended things with you.'

'This situation is entirely different.'

'Different how?'

'You're being an idiot.'

Lily gaped, the tears receding as indignation took over. 'Excuse me?'

'Well, you are.'

'I can't trust the man I love. I'm heartbroken.'

'That's just it.'

'That's just what?'

'All this nonsense about you not being able to trust Kit is rubbish.'

Rubbish? *Rubbish?* 'It isn't rubbish,' said Lily mutinously. 'It's the crux of the matter. The defining feature of our relationship. Ex-relationship.'

Zoe eyed her shrewdly. 'So go on, then, tell me, what has he done to make you not trust him?'

'You know what he did.'

'I mean recently. Since you got back together again.'

Lily thought about it for a moment, racked her brains and riffled through her memory. And then frowned. 'Well, nothing, I guess.' The opposite, in fact. He'd gone so far out of his way to show her that she could trust him that he was practically in another country.

'Right. I see. So basically Kit made one lousy, brief mistake five years ago and you're still punishing him for it?'

'I'm not.'

'Then what are you doing?'

'The only thing I can,' said Lily, reiterating the mantra that had kept her more or less upright this last fortnight. 'Being sensible. Protecting myself. Surviving.'

'And how's that working out?'

'Not brilliantly,' she had to admit. 'But what else do you suggest?'

'A good long look in the mirror.'

Lily shuddered. 'I did that earlier. Got quite a fright.'

'Look deeper.'

Lily took a sip of wine and sighed. 'What are you getting at, Zoe? And no more cryptic stuff because my brain really can't take it at the moment.'

'What I mean is that you weren't exactly fault free in what happened all those years ago, were you?'

'I know that.'

'Yet when he suggested trying again Kit trusted that you'd have changed, didn't he? So why can't you trust that he has? Seems to me that's not very fair.'

Lily opened her mouth to say something, then closed it again because for one thing here was the waiter with their fish and chips and for another she didn't know what to say to that. Still hadn't figured out an answer by the time the waiter had brought cutlery and condiments and had then retreated.

'And actually,' continued Zoe, picking up the ketchup and squeezing a dollop on the side of her plate, 'if anyone's had their trust broken it seems to me that it's Kit, because from your description of the way things were going before you broke up it sounds like, unlike him, you haven't changed at all.'

Zoe dipped a chip in the ketchup and popped it in her mouth while all Lily could do was stare at her. 'What?'

'You've been doing that tortoise thing again, haven't you?'

'What tortoise thing?'

'The pulling yourself into your shell and hiding while life and its problems go on around you.'

At her sister's bluntness Lily bristled. 'If that was what I was doing, and I'm not saying it was, don't you think it would be understandable? Don't you think some kind of self-defence would be normal?'

'There's no "if" about it,' said Zoe. 'You *have* been doing that, and, self-defence or not, it's a mistake. One you're consciously making.'

Lily looked at her sister in frustration, because Zoe might be all loved-up at the moment, but did she really think it was that simple? Could she really not see how hard it had been for her to end their relationship? How heart-broken she was by what she'd had to do? Did Zoe really think she'd made a mistake by wanting to protect herself from the kind of pain that had torn her apart once before?

Had she really not changed at all?

'I can't just tell myself to trust him and, hey, that's that,' she said, beginning to feel a bit confused because she'd been so convinced she *had* changed.

'Why not?'

'Because it doesn't work like that.'

'Yes, it does.'

'How?' Because she'd dearly love to know.

'Some things, like love, can't be switched on and off,' said Zoe, picking up her knife and fork and levelling her a look, 'but trust isn't one of them. Trust is a choice you can make, Lily, and I think you should think very carefully about the one you've made because Kit's the best thing that's ever happened to you and if you don't sort out what you want and fix things you could blow it for good.'

As Zoe turned her attention to her fish Lily took a sip of wine and tried to unravel all the thoughts that were now churning round in her head.

Was her sister right? Was she still punishing Kit for what he'd done all those years ago? Had she been hiding from everything again? Was she making a mistake? Could she trust him?

As the answers she'd never have expected filtered into

her head the foundations of everything she'd been convinced of recently began to crack.

Maybe she was still punishing him, she thought, her throat tightening as her heart thumped. Apart from that one brief moment, that complete aberration, Kit was the most reliable man she'd ever known. The most sincere. The most loyal. Yes, he'd had a one-night stand but he'd come clean immediately afterwards. Regretted it ever since, he'd said. He might have cheated but he hadn't lied. He'd always been totally honest with her. Been so open he was practically transparent.

But she hadn't been, had she? She'd asked for openness from him but she hadn't reciprocated. Instead she'd gone into denial. Unable to cope with what she was feeling, she'd shied away from it instead of confronting it. And then she'd run away like a coward in case she got hurt again.

Right now, though, the only person hurting her was herself and that was something she could fix because Zoe was right. Trust *was* a choice she could make and there was no one more deserving of it than Kit.

She'd been such a fool. She'd had no reason not to trust him, a billion reasons why she should and why she could, and instead she'd allowed herself to take the easy way out and run away, while he'd abandoned his pride and almost begged her to reconsider.

'What if I already have blown it, Zoe?' she said, shame and regret making her voice hoarse.

In the process of stabbing a piece of her fish with her fork Zoe stilled, glanced up and said, 'Then I suggest you make your way PDQ to the Fitness Rules gym next to Kit's hotel, where I happen to know he and Dan are playing squash, and unblow it.'

CHAPTER FIFTEEN

'WELL, THAT WAS quite a game,' said Dan, rubbing his neck and wincing as he rolled his shoulders. 'I'm not sure I'm ever going to recover.'

Feeling a stab of guilt, Kit wiped the sweat off his forehead and then threw the towel round his neck. 'Sorry,' he muttered, gloomily reflecting that if he'd known he was going to take his mood out on his squash partner he'd have cancelled this afternoon's game. Probably should have cancelled it anyway because maintaining a friendship with a man who was soon to be Lily's brother-in-law was hardly conducive to his intention to move on, however much he liked him.

'Not a problem,' said Dan easily. 'I can take losing once in a while. You look like hell by the way.'

'Thanks.'

'Anything you want to talk about?'

'Not particularly,' said Kit, stuffing his racket into its case and then slinging his bag over his shoulder.

'Right. Good.' Dan picked up his own bag and together they walked from the court in the direction of the changing rooms. 'So I heard that you and Lily had split up,' he said conversationally and the pain that shot through Kit made his breath catch.

'Yeah,' he said casually, as if it didn't rip his heart to shreds just to think about it.

'Want to know how she is?'

Desperately. 'I couldn't care less.'

'No. Right. Well, I guess that's understandable seeing as how she dumped you.'

Kit flinched and ruthlessly obliterated the sudden memory of that night in the garden when he hadn't been able to fix things.

'But if you did,' Dan continued, 'I'd have to tell you that she's a heartbroken wreck. Zoe's words, not mine. I'd also have to tell you that she looks like death warmed up. But you don't care, so I won't.'

At the knowledge that Lily sounded as miserable as he was, Kit felt something inside him collapse. All that drivel about wiping her from his life and his heart, probably, because who had he been kidding? There was absolutely zero chance of that happening.

Grinding his teeth against his pathetically weak willpower when it came to Lily, Kit gave in to the need to talk to someone and maybe get a different take on the situation because he hadn't exactly been doing brilliantly on his own. 'Did you know she doesn't think she can trust me?' he said, dumping his things on a bench and sitting down in case his limbs gave out.

'I had heard.'

'Any thoughts as to what I can do about that?'

'No idea. Can she trust you?'

'Yes.'

'Have you tried telling her?' Dan asked, opening his locker and taking out a towel before stashing his bag and racket.

'Many times and at length. It didn't make any difference.'

'Do you want her?'

'More than I want my next breath,' said Kit. 'But five

years ago I did something stupid. Something I've regretted ever since.'

'I heard about that too.'

'And it's turned out to be too great an obstacle to overcome.'

'So we all make mistakes,' said Dan, now armed with a bottle of shower gel as well as a towel.

'This was some mistake.'

'Yeah, but it was a while ago, wasn't it?'

'Five years.'

'And has Lily never made a mistake?'

Kit frowned as all the mistakes she'd made filtered into his head. 'Plenty.'

'So stop beating yourself up and do something about it. Marry her or something. Bind her to you so she can't escape and prove it over and over again until she has no choice but to trust you. Bit drastic, I know, but what else are you going to do?'

As Dan strode off and shut himself in one shower cubicle Kit stashed his things in his locker, grabbed a towel and headed for another, his mind beginning to race.

Was Dan right? he wondered, turning on the tap and feeling hot needles of water pummelling his skin. Was he beating himself up unnecessarily about the mistake he'd made? Had he let Lily dictate the way things had gone out of some kind of sense of inadequacy? Had that been totally the wrong thing to do?

Maybe it had, because Lily wasn't perfect, was she? For the last few weeks he'd been tearing himself apart with remorse and guilt over what he'd done, but what about Lily? Hadn't she reverted to type when the going had got tough? She had. And while he'd made huge changes and sacrifices for them she'd hardly done a thing.

So maybe he wasn't blame free in their break-up this time round, but neither was she. Just like before. They were equals. They always had been. Which meant that he *was* worthy of her, dammit. He *did* deserve her. They deserved each other.

He shouldn't have let her get away with ending things between them, he thought, turning off the water and grabbing his towel. That had been a mistake. One he wouldn't be making again because he loved her and she loved him and he was, well, he was wasting time.

Having abandoned Zoe in the pub after her sister had told her to go and then heading straight to the gym, Lily didn't have a plan. She hadn't had the time to formulate one. Nor had she had the mental space because her head was so full to the brim with the realisation of what a foolish idiot she'd been and her heart was pounding with so much love and hope and regret at the way she'd behaved that there wasn't room for anything else.

So when she pushed through the door of the gym and saw Kit striding purposefully across the lobby for a split second she didn't know what to do. For a moment she just watched him, her heart swelling because he looked so gorgeous, so familiar, and she loved him so damn much.

He also looked like she felt. Drawn. Haggard. Unkempt. As though basic self-maintenance was simply too great a challenge to face these days. Which was something of a boost to her pretty shaky confidence because if he'd looked clean-shaven and crisp, as if he hadn't been pining for her the way she had for him and was totally over her, she'd have been straight out of the door.

As it was, when he saw her he stopped dead, stared at her, his face totally unreadable, and she didn't know whether he was glad to see her or surprised or appalled. All she knew was that her heart was thundering so loudly it was a miracle no one else seemed to be able to hear it and her body was straining to throw itself at him and she wasn't going anywhere.

Literally. However hard it was she was staying right where she was because there'd be no throwing of anything anywhere until she'd said what she had to say, whatever that was.

'Hello, Kit,' she said, aiming for breezy nonchalance but, she suspected, failing.

His brows snapping together in a frown, Kit stalked over to her and stopped about a metre away. 'You're here,' he said.

'So it would seem,' she said, a bit breathless as her lungs were having trouble functioning in his presence.

'Why?'

'I wanted to talk.'

'Seems to be the fashion at the moment.'

'What?'

'Never mind,' he muttered.

'I thought we could go to your hotel. Maybe a meeting room or something.' Not his apartment though. No. Way too many disturbing and distracting memories there.

'Good idea,' he said, taking her arm and wheeling her round. 'You'd better come with me.'

He marched her out of the gym at such a rate that she had to jog to keep up. He held her tight as he led her into his hotel and across the lobby and she tried not to respond to the feel of him that she'd so badly missed. When he bypassed the ground-floor meeting rooms and took her to the lift she protested but her protest went unnoticed.

By the time they reached his apartment Lily was out of breath and her stomach was fluttering because Kit had a kind of energy about him, a sizzling sort of tension and a sense of purpose that she'd never seen before and it was doing crazy things to her heart.

He dropped his things on a chair, then thrust his hand

deep into the pockets of his jeans and turned to face her. At the fire in his eyes and the intensity of his expression, Lily's knees nearly gave way and a flicker of hope at the thought that she might not have screwed things up for good began to burn deep inside her.

Kit raked his gaze over her. 'Dan was right,' he said flatly. 'You do look awful.'

'So do you.'

'Yes, well, I feel it.'

'Me too.'

'But I'm glad you're here,' he said, flashing her a quick, lethal smile.

Oh, thank goodness for that, she thought, letting out a breath of relief because he was acting so oddly she hadn't been sure. 'You are?'

Kit nodded. 'Saves me a journey.'

'Where were you going?'

'To come and find you.'

Lily felt her heart turn over and that little flame of hope began to burn a little more fiercely. 'Oh.'

'So my carbon footprint thanks you.'

'It's welcome. But now can I tell you what I came to say?' she said, feeling so encouraged by the fact that he hadn't ignored her or turned her away that she was now practically exploding with the need to fix what she'd done.

'In a moment,' he said. 'Sit down.'

'I don't want to sit down.'

'Sit.'

She sat, even more bemused and now quite a bit more turned on by his dark, edgy demeanour. 'Are you all right, Kit?' she asked, leaning forwards and looking at him closely. 'You seem, I don't know, a bit weird.'

'I'm fine.'

'Sure,' she murmured, and then couldn't quite remember what she'd been thinking because Kit was fixing her with a look that had her heart thumping and her mouth going dry and her head swimming.

'OK, so here's the thing, Lily,' he said, and for some reason she shivered. 'Despite what happened a fortnight ago, we are not over.'

As his words hit her poor, battered brain her heart tripped and then swelled to bursting. 'You have no idea how glad I am to hear you say that, because—'

But he held up his hand and cut her off. 'Let me finish. I love you, Lily, but you are as far from perfect as I am.'

'Oh, you're so right,' she said with heartfelt conviction. 'I'm not perfect at all.'

'And, yes, I made a mistake but it was years ago and I refuse to carry the guilt around any longer.'

'Good, well, about that—'

'You've made many more mistakes than I have.'

She nodded. 'I know, I know.' She'd made tons.

'I thought I wasn't worthy of you. But I am.'

For a moment she reeled. How could he ever have thought that? Had *she* made him think that? 'You are,' she said with a stab of shame.

'We need each other, Lily,' he said, his eyes dark and intense and focused wholly on her. 'We love each other and we deserve each other.'

'We do.'

'So here's how this is going to go. We're going to get married, you and I, after which I plan to devote the rest of my life to proving to you how much you can trust me. We're going to communicate. Talk. Be a proper partnership. We're also going to adopt a brood of children and be extremely happy.' He arched an eyebrow as if challenging her to object. 'So what do you think about that?'

But why would she object when it was everything she wanted? Filled with so much relief, happiness and love she couldn't speak, instead Lily just walked over to him, put her arms around his neck, pressed herself against him and kissed him.

And damn it felt good because it had been such a long, miserable time since she'd been in his arms, but now she was because he was hauling his hands out of his pockets and putting them on her back, pulling her tight to him and kissing her back equally fiercely.

Free from all the insecurities that had plagued her these last few weeks, all the doubt and confusion that had so troubled her, and filling with the absolute certainty that she and Kit were going to be all right, she kissed him long and hard and with everything she felt. And when they broke for breath, his breathing was as ragged as hers, his heart was thundering as hard and fast as hers and his eyes were blazing as fiercely as she could imagine hers were.

'I'm taking it that you're not averse to the idea,' he said hoarsely.

'I couldn't be more for it,' she said with a giddy kind of smile. 'Although that bit about devoting the rest of your life to proving to me how much I can trust you? You don't need to do that.'

He frowned. 'I don't? Why not? I was looking forward to it.'

'I don't know how I could ever have thought I couldn't trust you, Kit. I'd trust you with my life. I'm so sorry for doubting it.'

'You trust me?' he said after a moment's pause. 'Since when?'

'Since about an hour ago.'

'What happened an hour ago?'

'I came to realise that trust is a choice, and I guess before I chose not to trust you. I don't exactly know why. Because I was scared maybe? Because it was all going too fast and I panicked? Because I could feel myself retreating and I couldn't stop it?'

'And now?'

'Now I want to trust you and I do. With everything I am and everything I have, because when have you given me reason to doubt it? You haven't. Not once. And you won't. I know that.' She shook her head in despair. 'I was such a fool. I went back on our deal to communicate and shut you out again. But I promise that that won't happen again because I'm done with denial. It's the coward's way out and I don't want to be a coward any more. I'm sorry if I made you think you don't deserve me because if anything I don't deserve you. And I'm sorry for breaking up with you. It was just about the worst thing I could have done. This last fortnight has been horrible. The worst of my life.'

'Mine too,' said Kit, his voice rough. 'I thought I'd lost you for good.'

'No, no,' she said, 'I was the one doing the losing.'

He tilted his head and looked down at her, his eyes filled with warmth and love and the promise of a future. 'I'm pretty sure it was me, but do you really want to argue about this?'

'Not really.'

He gave her a soft smile and his eyes took on a gleam. 'Because you know there are far better things we could be doing,' he said, his hands slowly sweeping up her back to her shoulders and making her shudder with longing.

'Like what?'

'Like you agreeing to marry me. Will you?'

Lily felt the backs of her eyes begin to prickle because how many people got a second chance? How many people were that lucky? 'Yes,' she said, blinking a bit. 'Because I want to, obviously, not because you scared me into it with all that "this is how it's going to go" thing.'

Kit's smile deepened and what with the way he was now stroking the skin of her shoulders her stomach practically dissolved. 'I'm sorry about that,' he murmured. 'But I wasn't taking any chances.'

'Don't be,' she said breathlessly. 'It was very assertive. Very dynamic. Very alpha male.'

'I'm delighted you think so.'

'And attractive.'

He slid his hands beneath the spaghetti straps of her vest top and slowly inched them down. 'How attractive exactly?' he asked softly.

'Extremely,' she said, beginning to tremble.

'So about these other things we could be doing...'

* * * * *

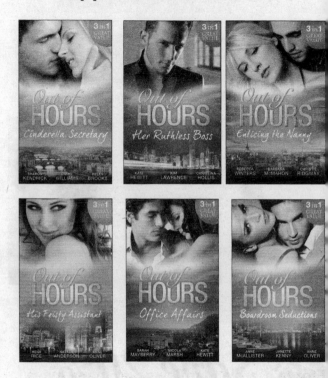

Discover more romance at

www.millsandboon.co.uk

- ❤ WIN great prizes in our exclusive competitions
- ❤ BUY new titles before they hit the shops
- ❤ BROWSE new books and REVIEW your favourites
- ❤ SAVE on new books with the Mills & Boon® Bookclub™
- ❤ DISCOVER new authors

PLUS, to chat about your favourite reads, get the latest news and find special offers:

- 🅕 Find us on facebook.com/millsandboon
- 🐦 Follow us on twitter.com/millsandboonuk
- ❤ Sign up to our newsletter at millsandboon.co.uk

M&B_WEB